# Ribbons in Her Hair

Colette McCormick

Published by Accent Press Ltd 2018
Octavo House
West Bute Street
Cardiff
CF10 5LJ

www.accentpress.co.uk

ISBN 9781786155429
eISBN 9781786155412

Printed and bound in Great Britain by Clays Ltd,
Elcograf S.p.A

For my mum and my sister
the women who put ribbons in my hair

## SUSAN

One of my first memories is of coming out of school when I was about five or six and seeing my mum waiting for me at the school gates. It was a sunny day and she was wearing a red cardigan. It has been more years than I care to remember, but I can still see her there at those paint-chipped gates, standing out from the other mothers in her red cardigan. It wasn't that she was prettier than the others, or that her clothes were better, that made her stand out from the rest. What made her stand out was that she was my mum and she was waiting for me.

Mum didn't like waiting for anything and I don't think she liked taking me to school either. She took me every morning and picked me up every afternoon; ten minutes there and then ten minutes back, that's all it was, but it was like it was an inconvenience to her – time wasted that she could have better spent doing something else.

In the morning she was always in a rush to get me to school because she 'had things to do,' and in the afternoon it was the same because she had to get home to 'get the tea on'. Sometimes I would have to run just to keep up with her.

When I looked at the other mothers with their children I had a feeling inside me that I didn't understand. I would look at them and think *why can't we hold hands*? Or, *why don't you talk to me*? And I would have this feeling in my chest. I now know that feeling was jealousy, the old green-eyed monster, but back then I just knew that it made me feel sad.

As soon as we got home from school she would tell me to go upstairs and get out of my school uniform, and she would disappear into the kitchen to get the tea on.

I once heard her say to one of the neighbours that my dad had never come home from work, and not had a meal waiting for him and I think that was probably right. When she wasn't in the kitchen cooking, Mum would be cleaning something. Thinking about it now, there was always a lovely smell in our house, one that I can only describe as the smell of clean – well, cleanliness; that floral disinfectant smell of a room that's just been cleaned – though it was probably more carbolic than floral back in those days. Mum was very house proud, the house always sparkled, and like I said, Dad's tea was always ready when he got in from work. Dad worked in a factory and Mum's job was to be the perfect housewife, and you had to hand it to her, she was good at her job; she was the perfect housewife. She just wasn't much of a mother.

Mum would get on with her chores and I would sit, usually in my bedroom so I wouldn't make the living room untidy, and play on my own. I sometimes thought she forgot I was there at all and maybe that was what she wanted; you know, if she ignored me long enough I might go away.

She treated all three of us the same though, it wasn't like she singled me out. Helen and Julie were my older sisters and Mum didn't show them any affection either.

Helen was eleven years older than me, so by the time I was old enough to go to school she was at the other end of her school life and had already moved on. She went to college to learn short-hand and typing. I didn't really know what either of those things were but Helen used to say that they'd mean she could get a good job and get away from 'this place'. Sometimes after college she used to go out with her friends and Mum would ask her if there had been any boys there. Helen always said that there hadn't been but I sometimes heard her and Julie whispering about a boy called John, though they'd always shut up when they realised I was there.

Julie was two years younger than Helen and went to 'Big School'. Julie talked about boys a lot. When she was going to do her exams Mum said that she needed to forget about boys and concentrate on her school work.

3

'What for?' Julie used to ask, 'I'm going to be a hairdresser and you don't need qualifications for that.'

'Never mind hairdressing,' Mum would say, 'you could stop on.'

But Julie didn't want to stop on. Julie hated school and couldn't wait to leave.

So you see, for all there were three of us, in a lot of ways I was like an only child. My sisters were moving on to college and work and I was a little girl just starting school. I didn't understand anything about their world and they didn't appear to want to know anything about mine. We didn't even look alike. Anyone could see that they were sisters; they were tall and blonde, slim and pretty, while I was short and fat and had mousy hair. Mum used to say that I was 'big boned' because God forbid that anyone in the family should be fat, but I knew what I was and that was chubby at best.

You know how some things from your childhood stick in your mind? Well, the thing that really sticks in my mind is that my mum never did pretty things with my hair. I don't even remember her washing it, let alone plaiting it or putting it in ponytails. Thinking about it now she must have washed it when I was very young, or someone must have, but I don't remember it. I only ever remember washing my own hair. And that was fine but why didn't Mum brush my hair and tie

4

pretty ribbons in it? All the other girls in my class used to have their plaits and ponytails tied up in gingham ribbons, but not me. My hair used to hang around my ears like rats' tails. The only time that Mum ever combed it was when I scratched my head and she put the nit comb through it.

I didn't mind the nit comb really. I mean it hurt – good God it hurt. Over and over again she'd dig it into my scalp and scrape it down but at least I was sitting close to my mum and we were doing something together...

'She'll not have nits,' Helen once told her. 'They only like clean hair.'

But Mum wasn't having any of it and just dug the metal teeth deeper into my scalp. 'They don't,' she said, 'Sandra Coogan's always getting nits and you can't tell me that she's clean. I went to school with her mother and she never knew what to do with a bar of soap.'

At the time, the comment meant nothing to me, it was just a comment – what I thought was a statement of fact. Years later, when I recalled the memory, it hurt and I wondered why Helen had said what she did. It's funny how the little things stick in your head.

Mum's comment about Sandra Coogan not being clean didn't make sense to me either because Sandra's hair was always tied up in a yellow ribbon. Well, apart from the times

5

that the nit nurse put that purple stuff on her head anyway. But at least she had ribbons sometimes. I never had ribbons in my hair.

Thank God I never had to have my head painted purple though. The shame would have killed Mum.

When I was about nine, Mum got a job. It was the first job that she'd had since she'd been married and she seemed happier than I'd ever seen her. She worked in a shop that sold just about everything from nails to fancy chandeliers, and her boss was called Mr Willis. I liked Mr Willis. He used to wink at me and call me 'flower'.

'You'll come home after school with Maggie next door,' Mum said when she dropped me off at the school gates on her first day at work.

That surprised me because Mum used to say that Maggie's mum was a 'filthy cow' and she didn't like me and Maggie playing together. I didn't mind though because we were in the same class and we often played together in the yard at break time.

I liked coming home with Maggie and her mum. Maggie's mum used to walk between us so that she could hold hands with both of us. Sometimes we used to skip. Then when we got back to their house we played together until Mum picked me up when she'd finished work.

6

Every night Mum asked the same question. 'Has she behaved herself?'

And every night Maggie's mum replied, 'Good as gold.'

In the summer after I left junior school, Maggie's dad got a job in another part of the country and they moved away. I cried the day they left and Mum told me to stop being such a baby. Maggie and I should have been going to Big School together, but instead I went alone.

Big school – well, comprehensive school – now there was an eye opener. None of the girls in my new school wore ribbons in their hair. Instead they wore make-up.

Helen and Julie wore make-up which I wasn't allowed to touch and Mum wore make-up when she and dad went out on a Saturday night, but before that first day at comprehensive school I didn't know of any girls my age that wore it. They probably shouldn't have been wearing it either because Miss Marshall, the form teacher, made them take it off and told them that if they wore it again they would be sent home.

I just thought that they all looked really pretty.

And the first day that we did PE I noticed that they all wore bras too. They were tiny little lacy things that covered up their non-existent breasts, so you can imagine my embarrassment as they all laughed at my vest when I took my blouse off.

'Can I have a bra?' I asked Mum that night.

'You don't need one,' she said and that was the end of the subject.

I think I was in the second year before I got one and it wasn't lacy like the ones that the other girls in my class wore. It was what I now think of as a 'utility' bra. You know the type, plain white with a full cup: boring, but at least it wasn't a vest.

I remember it was just after I got my first bra that I caught Helen and Julie talking about me. At first, I didn't know it was me they were talking about. They were in the kitchen and I was just the other side of the door, about to push it open, when I heard Helen say, 'I feel sorry for the poor little cow.' I was curious as to who they were talking about so I leaned towards the door and hoped to hear more. I was wondering who the 'poor little cow' was when I heard Julie say, 'I know. It's not Susan's fault that Mum didn't want any more kids,' and I realised they were talking about me.

I crept away and wished I hadn't heard what I had; apparently it was true what they said about eavesdroppers. I backed away from the door, being as quiet as I could. I didn't want them to know I had heard what they were saying. I went up to my bedroom and lay down on the bed. I cried for a long time. I don't know if anyone noticed that I wasn't around, but no one mentioned it so I suspect that they didn't.

I lay on my bed and played out what I had heard over and over again in my head. So Mum apparently hadn't wanted me. Well that might explain a lot of things. But when all was said and done, she was my mum and despite everything, I loved her. All I wanted was for her to love me back. All I wanted was for her to put her arms around me and give me a hug, or just to show me a bit of attention.

Now that I was at comprehensive school I was given a key for the front door. I don't think Mum liked the idea of me sitting on the doorstep after school waiting for her to get home from work. In one way I liked it because I felt grown up, but at the same time I hated it because I disliked going home to an empty house, even if it was only for an hour or so.

I sat next to a girl called Felicity Marsden in History and she was always going on about how her mum had a glass of milk and a piece of cake waiting for her when she got home from school. Her mum didn't have a job and was always there. I never told her that I let myself in to an empty house or that my mum worked in a shop.

I think I was about twelve years old when Helen brought Robert home for the first time. She had been going out with him for a while but that was the first time any of us were going to meet him.

Mum gave the house an extra special clean that day, not that there was any need because dust never got the chance to settle. 'He's from Grove Road,' Mum said, 'and his dad wears a suit to work so he'll be used to the best. We don't want to let Helen down because if she's bringing him home it must be serious.'

And it was serious because not long after that they announced that they were getting engaged and planned on getting married just after Christmas. Helen wanted me and Julie to be her bridesmaids.

Mum was over the moon. Helen was going up in the world, or at least that's what she said. I just thought that she was marrying someone that she loved. When Mum told anyone about the wedding, and God knows she told everyone, she always made a point of saying that they were getting married ten months after they were engaged.

I think Helen was embarrassed by that.

In those days it was the responsibility of the bride's parents to pay for the wedding so I imagine Mum was quite pleased when the happy couple announced that they wanted a 'small, intimate' affair. Dad worked overtime every minute that he could and Mum had to save every penny because the reception was going to be in a proper hotel and it was going to cost a small fortune.

Mum bought a twinset for the wedding and Dad had his suit made to measure.

One day, Mum was talking to Mrs Williams as they were both hanging out washing. Mrs Williams and her husband had moved into the house that Maggie and her family used to live in and, not for the first time, Mum was telling Mrs Williams about the wedding. She was carrying the empty basket back into the house and had just mentioned the colour of the hat she had bought when I heard her say, 'Mick always gets his suits made to measure.'

That struck me as odd because as far as I knew Dad didn't have another suit.

Helen had decided that the bridesmaids should wear pale pink. She said that it would suit our colouring. I don't know if it did or it didn't but I know that it suited Julie a lot better than me. But it was Helen's day and whatever Helen wanted she got, even down to little bags of sugared almonds as presents for the guests. Mum said wasn't it the guests that were supposed to bring them presents but Helen told her that when Robert's sister got married the guests had all been given little gifts so that was that. If it was good enough for the insurance man's daughter, it was good enough for hers.

Despite what Helen had said, pale pink really wasn't my colour but it didn't matter what I was wearing because nobody paid me any attention anyway. Not that that bothered me because I didn't particularly want to be noticed. I'd looked in the mirror; I knew what I looked like.

Robert's mum said that I looked nice but I knew that she was just being polite. In fact, she was very polite to all of my family.

I think that it was around that time that I thought about decorating my bedroom. I asked if I could paint the walls yellow but Mum said that she liked them the colour they were. I couldn't understand that. There was nothing to like about white; it wasn't really a colour at all.

I contented myself with covering most of the walls with posters. I don't think Mum liked the idea of the holes in the walls from the drawing pins but she said that Blu Tack would peel the paper off, so holes were the lesser of two evils.

That room should have been my haven and I'd just wanted to make it – I don't know – an extension of myself, I suppose. Even though everyone still treated me like a child my body was developing and I was becoming a young woman and I had reached the stage in my life where I needed a space of my own. I wanted a private place and I assumed that my bedroom was going to be it.

Mum had other ideas. She would often wander into my room while I was in there and as if that wasn't bad enough, she did it when I wasn't. I didn't even think about it when I was very young but, as I got older, her just going into my room really irritated me. I was always finding things had been moved. It seemed that I couldn't even arrange my own things in my own bedroom the way I wanted them.

I mentioned it to Mum one day but she said she thought the room looked better set out the way she had done it. End of discussion. I could have moved my things back the way I had had them, but there seemed little point because Mum would only have moved them back again. Even my bed had to be made the way that she wanted it: every morning I made my bed and every day Mum made it again.

'Ignore it,' Julie said to me one day, 'it's just her way.'

Everything had to be Mum's way.

Less than a year after Helen got married, Julie announced that she was getting married too. She hadn't known Christopher very long but she said that it was, 'the real thing'. I was about fourteen then and although some of the girls at school had boyfriends I wasn't one of them. I had no idea what 'the real thing' felt like. To be honest I didn't know what anything felt like. Looking back I think my early years just seemed to have passed me by.

I could tell that Mum wasn't very happy about Julie's plans. She didn't actually tell me she wasn't but it was obvious. There was none of the excitement that had surrounded Helen's wedding. I guess Mum didn't think that Julie was going up in the world by the marriage she was making.

Despite Mum's reservations Julie was determined that she was going to get married and that being the case there was a proper way to do things, so Mum set the wheels in motion. I think that she was scared Julie would carry out her threat to run away and get married or worse still, to just live with Christopher and not get married at all.

I was over the moon when Julie asked me if I'd like to go with her and Mum to look at wedding dresses. I'll always remember that day as a happy one. Julie asked me for my opinion and she seemed interested in what I had to say.

We'd already looked at a few dresses when Julie asked me what I thought of the one in her hand. It was an ivory-coloured, fifties style dress with a tight, off the shoulder bodice, a pinched in waist and a skirt that would finish around Julie's calves. Delicate lace of a slightly darker shade than the dress would cover her neck and shoulders. It was the most gorgeous thing that I had ever seen in my life.

'You should wear a pill box hat with it,' I told her. I don't know where that idea came from because me and fashion were not happy bedfellows but Julie seemed to like it.

I remember a smile spreading over Julie's face. 'I should,' she said.

She gave me a hug. I don't ever remember being hugged before and it felt good.

Mum came towards us with a meringue-shaped dress in her hand. 'Here's one,' she said.

'It's all right Mum,' Julie told her, 'I've found the one I want.' Julie held the hanger up to her chin so that the dress rested on her body. 'Isn't it gorgeous?' she said, 'And Susan suggested that I wear a pill box hat. It'll be great.'

Mum looked horrified. 'No.'

'But I want this one.'

'No you don't.'

'I do, Mum.'

'No.'

'But with the pill box hat it'll be perfect.'

'I've already asked your Aunty Anne if you can borrow Josephine's veil so you don't need one that'll go with a pill box hat. This dress will go nicely with the veil.'

Mum took the dress from Julie and hung it on the nearest rail. It was as though the dress had offended her in some way. Both Julie and I knew that it wasn't the dress that Mum objected to, it was the colour.

'But Mum, loads of people get married in ivory,' Julie pleaded.

'Not my daughter,' Mum said without looking at her.

Julie reluctantly conceded defeat and that she would be married in the white meringue dress that our mother had chosen, wearing Cousin Josephine's veil on her head.

'It doesn't matter,' she said to me as Mum paid for the dress. 'I'm getting married and that's the main thing.'

I tried to be cheerful for her but I could tell that she was disappointed. She was right about it not mattering though because she would have looked good in whatever she wore.

The night before Julie's wedding I was sitting on my bed leaning against the wall with my knees pulled up towards my chin when I was surprised by a gentle tapping on the bedroom door.

'Yes?' I said nervously. Nobody ever knocked at my bedroom door.

The door opened and Julie's head appeared. 'Can I come in?'

'Yes.' No one had ever asked if they could come into my room before either.

Julie came and sat on the bed with me and we chatted for a while. We talked about the wedding and she told me how happy she was and I told her that I was happy for her. Eventually Julie said that we had a big day ahead of us and that we should get an early night. She started to push herself off the bed then stopped and sat on the edge.

'Be strong, Susan,' she told me. 'You're going to need to be strong.'

I didn't have to ask her what she meant.

Things certainly didn't get better after Julie left but at least they didn't get any worse. A few months after the wedding Helen had a baby boy and Mum loved being a grandma. She knitted baby James more matinee coats than he'd ever be able to wear, and was determined to out do Robert's parents when it came to Christmas presents. I often wished that Helen would ask me to baby-sit but she never did.

I went to my first party when I was sixteen. One of the few girls that I called friends was going and wanted someone to go with her. I had to ask Mum for permission of course and was surprised when it was given.

17

The day before the party I went into town on my way home from school and bought some make-up. I applied eyeshadow for the first time in my life, a bit too heavily as I recall, and lip gloss that tasted of strawberries. Mum even let me spray on a little of her eau de toilette behind my ears. I can still remember that I wore a denim skirt and a cheesecloth blouse and hoped that I'd look all right compared to everyone else.

I thought that Mum almost smiled when she saw me ready to go out and she even told me to enjoy myself. Maybe she did want me to be happy after all.

Dad took me to the party and said he would pick me up afterwards which was a bit embarrassing as everyone else seemed to arrive either on their own or in a group, but it was a small price to pay.

I loved the dancing and talking and was amazed at what some of the girls allowed boys to do to them. I'd never even kissed a boy before so the thought of one of them putting their hand inside my blouse was unimaginable.

I was probably the first person to leave the party but I didn't want to keep Dad waiting. I know that some people laughed at me getting picked up by my dad but, as I said before, it was a small price to pay for being allowed to go. I'd had a wonderful time.

Mum was waiting for us. She asked me who had been at the party, what I had done and who I had talked to. I don't know why she didn't just ask me if I'd let a lad do anything to me – it was what she really wanted to know.

There were more parties after that first one and at last I started to feel as though I had a life. Mum even bought me some new clothes. She said that if I was going to be going to parties I would need them. They might not have been the clothes that I'd have chosen, well they definitely weren't, but they were okay. I'd rather she had given me some money so that I could buy my own, but beggars can't be choosers.

There was a party one Saturday, just before the Christmas before my seventeenth birthday, when a boy asked me to dance. It was the first time that had happened and even though it was such a long time ago I still remember exactly how it felt. My heart started to beat really fast and my breath got caught in my throat so that I could hardly speak. He led me into a space amongst the others that were dancing and I was bursting with happiness. As I hopped from foot to foot in time with the music I didn't know where to look. I was too shy to look at him because I knew that he was looking at me.

'What's your name?' he asked, leaning forward and shouting above the music.

'Susan,' I shouted back. 'What's yours?'

19

'Tony.'

When the music stopped and was replaced by something much slower I thought that the moment was over but I remember how Tony took my hand and pulled me towards him. I'd stood on the edge of dance floors watching the slow dances enough to know what I should do next and I'm giggling to myself as I recall that dance. We were just inches apart, moving from side to side, my hands on his shoulders and his on my waist. It was hardly ballroom.

Oh but he smelled so good. Pine I think. Pine like a forest, mind you, not disinfectant. Just kidding; it was really nice.

And as we danced I was aware that we were getting closer to each other and before I knew it our bodies were brushing against each other. Suddenly I felt his soft lips on my forehead, then on my nose and finally on my lips. My stomach did somersaults and I felt something that I had never felt before.

At the end of the night, after he'd kissed me one last time he asked if he could see me again the following week. I said that I would have to check that I wasn't doing anything and ring him. Maybe he thought that I was playing hard to get which, ironically, is a game that I've never got the hang of, but the truth is that I had to ask.

Mum said that I could go out but Tony would have to collect me from the house so that she could meet him. Thankfully he didn't mind.

I was officially going out with someone. For the first time in my life, and a couple of years after most of the girls I knew, I had a boyfriend.

Four months later Tony packed me in for another girl. I was absolutely heartbroken and cried myself to sleep. A couple of days later he turned up at the house when he knew that I'd be alone and told me how sorry he was that he had hurt me. He told me that part of him still loved me and probably always would. Stupidly I believed him and said yes when he asked if he could have sex with me. I thought that I loved Tony and just wanted him to love me back. I never saw Tony again after that day.

There was a series of boyfriends after that. None of them were serious or lasted more than a few weeks. None of them got any further than a fondle under my top. None of them asked for it to go any further but, if they had, I probably would have said yes because in my naïve little head I equated the physical contact with love. Plus I didn't want to be rejected again, and if I'd refused to do anything that they'd asked me to do they might have rejected me. The truth is that they all rejected me anyway and most of the time

21

I didn't care. I did enjoy being someone's girlfriend though. It made me feel normal. It meant someone liked me and wanted to be with me.

Then I met Tim through a mutual friend.

Okay, so I admit that his family were a bit rough, but at the end of the day we did live on the same estate as them so either they weren't as bad as Mum made out, or we were a lot worse than she liked to pretend. Anyway, he was just a boyfriend, a lad that I went out with. He took me to the pub and bought me a few drinks. Once he took me out for a meal which I thought was very grown up.

'You could do better,' Mum said one day while she was ironing and I was doing my homework at the kitchen table. I asked her what she meant. She put the iron down, looked at me and said. 'I mean that you could do better for yourself than Tim Preston.'

I nodded my head as if I was listening. Maybe she even thought that I was agreeing with her. The reality was that Tim Preston had suddenly become much more attractive. If I'm honest though, I never believed that we would spend the rest of our lives together and – as I'm trying to be completely honest here – I should probably admit that I wasn't really that keen on him at all. I just didn't want to be alone and he had asked me out. He even told me that he loved me, but only after he'd had a couple of pints. It's only looking back now that I can see that they were just words but at the time I thought that he meant it. To feel loved was all that I'd ever wanted.

One night when we were alone in his parent's house, a kiss and a cuddle on the sofa in the living room turned into something it shouldn't have, and before I knew it we were in his bedroom.

I'm not saying that he raped me because he didn't, he just didn't ask and I didn't tell him that I wanted him to stop. I let him do it. Six weeks later, I'd been dumped and I hadn't had a period. What's more, Mum knew that I hadn't had a period. Don't ask me how, she just did.

'How long is it since you were last on?' she asked.

'I don't know,' I said honestly. I really didn't know how long it had been. I just knew that it had been too long.

'Have you got something that you want to tell me?'

'No,' I said. Why would she think that I would want to tell her that I might be pregnant?

'Here, use this,' she said, throwing a box at me. It was a home pregnancy test.

I told her that I would do it the next morning.

It should have been a relief when the test was negative, and it was for a day or two, until Mum said that I should put another test in at the doctor's.

'Just to make sure,' she said.

The receptionist gave me a funny look when I passed over the little pot of pee but she didn't say anything. She'd seen it all before.

A few days later our family doctor apologised when he told me that I was pregnant.

## JEAN

I didn't let it happen just to trap Mick, why would I? I'd only known him for a couple of months for God's sake. No, I didn't set the trap, though I knew some that had. It wasn't my intention to get pregnant; it just happened.

My mam knew almost before I did. She didn't tell me that she knew, or how, but I could tell that she did. There was something about the way that she looked at me when she gave me a mug of tea one morning.

'What's wrong?' I asked her.

She just looked at me.

'What?'

She grabbed her coat and pushed her arms into it. It was a cold morning and she fastened it right up to the top. 'Don't go in to work today,' she said as she took her purse from the dresser drawer.

'Why?'

She slammed the door behind her.

I didn't go to work. I knew that there'd be bother when I went in the next day but there'd be even more trouble if I disobeyed Mam and I didn't need any more trouble.

When she came back she was carrying a brown paper bag. It had some stuff in it that she'd got from the chemist and she sat with me while I drank it. Foul tasting stuff it was and when I gagged Mam just held the bottle to my mouth and made me drink it all.

'If we're lucky, that'll put you right,' she said as she smashed the bottle and wrapped it in yesterday's newspaper before burying the evidence deep in the bin.

But it didn't work, so a few days later Mam put me in a bath of boiling water and gave me a bottle of gin to drink.

That didn't work either.

I sat at the kitchen table crying my eyes out while Mam stood opposite me with her arms folded across her chest.

'Don't be wasting time with them,' she said, 'tears are no good to you now.' Oh God, my mother was a hard woman; I sometimes wondered if she had a heart at all. She couldn't bring herself to look at me and stared out of the window instead. 'Your dad'll kill you and your brothers'll kill him.'

The thought of that just made me cry even harder.

'Shut your bloody crying, Jean,' she yelled at me. She pulled a chair from under the table and sat down. 'How could you be so stupid?'

All I wanted was for her to put her arms around me and tell me that everything was going to be all right. But she didn't, she just sat there and glared at me.

'I'm sorry,' I whispered.

'Too late for bloody sorry now.' She looked at me through her hard eyes. 'Well, I've tried everything I know,' she said eventually, 'but Mrs Walsh at the bottom of Hagg Lane might be able to do something.'

'No,' I screamed, 'Please Mam, no.' My friend Dorothy had nearly died when Mrs Walsh had got rid of her baby.

She carried on staring at me across the table as she chewed on her toothless gums.

'Well you know what you've got to do then, my girl,' she said as she got up from the table.

Mick was on the early shift and he'd be finished at four. If I hurried, I could be there when he came out of the factory.

\*\*\*

He came out of the gates with a couple of other blokes. One of them was Tom Bridges and I saw him say something to Mick and nod his head towards me. Mick gave him a playful punch on the arm. He was laughing as he came over to me.

'Hello, love,' he said.

I couldn't have spoken even if I'd wanted to but Mick didn't give me the chance.

27

'You should have heard what that cheeky get Tom said,' he laughed. 'He said that the only day that his lass ever met him out of work was the day that she told him she'd fallen wrong.'

He was still laughing as I burst into tears.

'What're you crying for?'

I just looked at him with tears pouring down my cheeks. And then the penny dropped.

'Fucking hell, you're not are you?'

All I could do was nod.

'Bollocks.'

'I'm sorry,' I stammered.

The colour drained from his face.

'Who've you told?' he asked.

'My mam.'

'What about your dad?'

I shook my head.

He looked at his feet and shoved his hands deep into his pockets. I watched him and waited. He shuffled his feet and started to nod his head slowly.

'What time's he get home?' he asked.

I didn't have to ask why he wanted to know.

'His shift finishes at six,' I told him, 'then he'll have a couple of pints. He usually gets home about half seven.'

'I'll come over,' he said before he walked away.

As I watched Mick go I realised that I was now tied to him forever. I also realised that I didn't like him half as much as I thought I had and I wondered why I had let him do those things to me in the back of that mucky van and twice behind the dance hall. But I knew really why I had: he'd paid me attention and that made me feel good. All I'd wanted was to feel loved.

I went home with a heavy heart.

'Well?' Mam turned from the stove as I walked into the kitchen.

'He's coming to see Dad tonight,' I told her as I looked at the chair Dad always sat in.

Mam turned back to whatever it was that she was cooking. 'You'd better hope he does,' she said, lifting a spoonful of God knows what to her mouth to taste. 'Because if he doesn't you know that the lads'll go looking for him.' She reached for the salt. 'And God help him if that happens.'

But my brothers didn't have to go looking for Mick. He turned up like he said he would to face my dad, to face up to his responsibilities.

Dad was sitting in his chair with a mug of tea in his hand and the newspaper on his knee. Mam was washing up and Thomas my eldest brother was sitting at the table finishing

29

his food. When Mick arrived Mam whipped Thomas's plate away from him and nodded her head towards the door. He was about to moan that he hadn't finished his tea but thought better of it when he saw the look on Mam's face. She left the room as well leaving me to let Mick in.

Dad didn't look up as he asked, 'What's all this about then?'

Mick stood in front of Dad and I stood beside him.

'Well?' Dad asked as he folded the newspaper and put it behind his back.

'Jean's having a baby.' Mick said.

'Is she now?' Dad pushed himself out of the chair and stood up.

Mick moved to stand in front of me though I don't know why because Dad would never have hit me. I thought for a second that he might hit Mick. Thank God he didn't because I don't think Mick would have taken it without hitting back.

Dad looked at Mick for a minute. Then he looked at me and all I could see was his disappointment.

Mick didn't stay long, half an hour at the most. In that time he had promised to do the right thing and make an honest woman of me. My shame would be covered up just as soon as possible, hopefully before I started to show. Personally I didn't understand what all the fuss was about. I mean, I knew that I would have to get married, but it wasn't like I was the first lass to fall wrong for God's sake – and I wouldn't be the last.

It wasn't the start to married life that I'd hoped for but I'd made my bed so I had to lie in it.

We were married in the local church a few weeks later. Mam bought me a white dress on the market. It wasn't what most people would have thought of as a wedding dress but there wasn't the time or the money for a traditional one. What I wore didn't matter though, I was getting married and that was the main thing. The dress was a bit tight but Mam made sure that I didn't show. How could I when I was wearing the girdle she'd bought me? I could barely breathe for God's sake and I held a little posy of flowers in front of me all the time. We had to hide my shame from the neighbours.

The wedding was a small family affair, just a few members of our immediate families at the church and then a reception in the back room of The Swan, the pub that my dad and brothers drank in. Mam had arranged for sandwiches and salad to be laid on and we even had a cake. It had to look like a regular wedding. The only thing missing was a fight, though it was touch and go for a while.

31

From the reception Mick and I made our way to his mam's house. Things being the way they were we couldn't get a place of our own. The wedding had been arranged so quickly that there hadn't been time to find anywhere and to be honest, we couldn't really afford it.

I felt a bit awkward going upstairs with Mick. It wasn't so much that I was in Mick's bedroom with its new double bed and the sheets that his mam had starched, it was more the fact that his parents and younger sister were sitting in the room below.

Mick didn't seem to mind though. He didn't seem to care who heard him.

***

It was hard being a wife to Mick while we were living in his mam's house. I never made my husband's tea and I never even ironed him a shirt. His mother still had her only son at home to look after and all she had to do to keep him there was put up with me, the tart that had trapped her son into marriage. I never felt comfortable around her.

I once tried to talk to my own mother about it but she wasn't interested. She said that I should be grateful. But I wasn't grateful; I was miserable.

My mother-in-law's name was Eileen but I never called her that. She was always 'Mick's mam'. Sometimes I would get up early in the hope that I would be able to make my husband his breakfast. But no matter what time I arrived in the kitchen Mick's mam was always there before me with a pot of tea brewing.

'Don't worry,' she would say with a smile – no, a smirk – on her face, 'I'll take care of our Mick. I know how he likes things.'

*Our* Mick. Wasn't he *my* Mick...? It was a small price to pay, I suppose, considering the alternative. If Mick hadn't married me I would have been ruined, and he could have walked away from it – from me. That had happened to more than one of the girls I went to school with. They had been left alone with their babies and not much hope of another man wanting them.

I just wished that Mick wouldn't leave me on my own with his mam so much. He knew that she didn't like me yet he still left me on my own with her. I know that he had to during the day when he was at work but why did he have to go to the pub every night? It was probably because his dad did and Mick was his father's son, or at least he wanted to be. I always felt he wanted to prove something to his dad; proving he was a man to his father was part of the reason behind a lot of things that Mick did.

They'd both come home from work and have their tea then, after a wash and a shave, they'd be off down the pub leaving me and my mother-in-law listening to the radio and knitting baby clothes.

I didn't like being pregnant and I wished I wasn't. If I hadn't been pregnant I wouldn't have been sitting, night after night, opposite a woman who hated me, working the needles to make clothes for a baby that I didn't want.

There. I've said it and it was true. I didn't want the baby that was growing in my belly. It wasn't just that I didn't want to be pregnant, I didn't want the heartburn or to be tired all the time either. I didn't want to be fat, and I certainly didn't want my tits to feel like balloons. I didn't want any of those things, but most of all, I didn't want my baby.

My baby was tying me to Mick and I didn't think I wanted that either. I was certain that Mick felt the same way. He didn't love me. He'd only married me because he'd not been careful enough. Everyone knew that we were going together so everyone would also know that my belly was his doing. He'd had to marry me, really. He'd had no choice. All that either of us could do was accept that things were the way they were. This was our life and we had to get on with it.

One day, when I was about eight months gone, I was in the town buying a few bits that Mick's mam wanted for tea. I was in the queue at the greengrocer's waiting to buy potatoes when I heard someone say my name. I turned around and saw Margaret Dobbs who I'd gone to school with. Except she wasn't called Dobbs any more; she'd married Bill Preston six months before her baby was born.

'Hello Margaret,' I said shifting my weight from leg to leg. I leaned over and looked into the pram that she was pushing. 'Who's this?'

'Billy,' she said, pushing the blanket that had been covering the baby down so that I could get a better look.

I stroked his cheek. 'Hello Billy,' I said. He was a cute enough little lad. We chatted for a minute or two and then I told her I had to get back with the shopping.

The potatoes were heavy and I walked slowly along the street, huffing and puffing with effort. It took me a long time to get back to the house.

'At last,' Mick's mam said when I walked through the door. 'I thought I was going to have to send out a search party.'

I didn't bother to answer her, I was too tired. I just went upstairs and lay on the bed.

Half an hour later my waters broke. I had to call for Mick's mam four times before she appeared at the bedroom door with an annoyed look on her face. Mick and his dad would be back from work in an hour and she was making their tea. She said as much when she opened the door, but when she saw what had happened she told me to put a nightgown on, climb into bed and relax while she went to fetch the nurse.

I lay in the bed alone and terrified. I watched the clock and waited for the nurse to arrive and wondered what was taking her so long. She arrived just as I was thinking that I might be going to die.

When Mick got home I wanted him with me but when I asked for him his mam said, 'What do you want him for? He's done his bit; it's your turn now.'

The nurse came close to me and put something cold on my forehead. Her face was close to mine and she stroked my hair. 'You're better off without him love,' she whispered. 'This is no place for a man – useless buggers,' and she smiled at me.

I wanted to smile back but another contraction came and I had to fight the pain that came with it.

Sometime during the night my baby was born. I lay in the bed and sobbed. I was so happy that it was over and that I had lived through it. I could hear my baby crying and just wanted it to shut up so that I could go to sleep, I was so tired.

I saw the nurse bringing it over to me. 'Your baby needs feeding,' she said.

I wanted to tell her to feed it herself then, but I knew that wasn't going to happen so I pushed myself up against the pillows and unbuttoned my nightgown. The nurse put my baby in my arms and showed me how to get it to take the breast. I looked down at the baby suckling on me and felt nothing. I started to cry and I know that the other women probably thought that it was with love for my newborn child, but really it was because I didn't know what was wrong with me. How could I not feel anything for this tiny creature in my arms that I had carried around inside me for all those months? I wanted to love it but I just didn't feel a thing.

The nurse must have sensed something because she came and sat on the edge of the bed and stroked my arm. 'Don't force it, Jean love,' she said. 'It'll come.'

I wanted to believe that she was right. I didn't want to hate the child that was the reason I was married to a man that I didn't love.

At last the baby was fed and had fallen asleep. The nurse took it from me and put it down in a cot that had somehow appeared by the side of the bed and then I fell asleep too.

When I woke up it was daylight and Mick was standing by the window with the baby in his arms. He was rocking it and talking to it. He looked happy.

I'd watched them for a couple of minutes before Mick sensed that I was awake. He turned around and looked at me in a way that he had never looked at me before. Maybe he did feel something for me after all.

'Hello,' he said, coming towards me with the baby in his arms. 'You all right?'

I nodded and maybe even smiled myself.

He sat on the bed close to my head. 'She's beautiful.'

And that's when it hit me that until that moment I hadn't known if I had a son or a daughter. I'd not even asked what I'd had. What sort of mother was I?

'What are we going to call her?' he asked without taking his eyes off his precious bundle.

I didn't know; I hadn't given it any thought.

'What about Helen?'

Why not, it was as good as anything. So I had a daughter called Helen.

And I tried to love her.

*** 

I have to say in my defence that I didn't neglect Helen. I fed her when she needed feeding and I cleaned up after her when she was dirty. I just didn't fuss over her twenty-four hours a day. Mick did enough of that for both of us anyway.

He didn't spend so long at the pub after Helen was born. He always made sure that he was home to spend at least a little time with his 'princess' before she went to bed. Mick loved being a father. He loved it so much that when Helen was only six months old he suggested, 'Let's have another one.'

Over my dead body, but Helen was less than eighteen months old when I knew that I was pregnant again. I still hadn't come round to wanting the baby that I already had and now I was having another. At least it meant that we would have to move out of Mick's mam's house. When we had two babies we would have to have our own place.

Thankfully we came to the top of the council list not long after I found out that I was expecting again and we were offered a two bedroom house on the same estate that our parents lived on. I snapped their hands off accepting it; I would be able to get the house just the way I wanted it before the baby came.

I loved that house. It was just a two up, two down, but it was mine. Well, it wasn't mine because it belonged to the council, but that didn't matter. Luckily for us, the people that had lived there before had been clean so we were able to move straight in without having to do much. I mean, I still scrubbed it from top to bottom but we didn't have to decorate it or anything. I had it looking like a palace by the time I was done.

I gave Mick another daughter and we called her Julie. I had hoped that this baby would be a boy: men always wanted a son, my mam always said that, and I'd only given my husband daughters. Which meant Mick might want me to go through it again...

Helen and Julie weren't bad girls. They had their moments, like any kids, but they weren't a bother really. And Mick seemed happy enough. He idolised his daughters and he was a good father. To be fair to him he was a good husband as well. He didn't knock me about, which is more than some of the lasses I knew could say. He worked hard and always provided for us. I didn't hate Mick but I didn't really love him either.

My mam always said that the reason you got married was to have children. I didn't want any more children. I knew that I would have to be careful about how I went about preventing another pregnancy – Mick could never know what I was doing.

I made sure that I never refused Mick though. I mean, I couldn't risk him looking elsewhere, could I? I didn't fancy

40

being left on my own with two kids. I'd seen that happen often enough to other people and I didn't like what I saw.

After a year or so, he started to get suspicious. He said that it was odd that I hadn't got pregnant again. 'We try often enough,' he laughed. Mick was very keen on that side of our marriage though, to be honest, I could have done without the bother.

I forced a smile and said that it would happen when it was meant to.

His mother mentioned it once at a family christening.

'Thought we'd have been having another one of these for you by now.'

'All in good time, Mam,' Mick said, 'all in good time.'

I fussed over the girls and hoped that no one could see the terror that I was feeling.

As the years went by without any additions to our family I started to believe that I wasn't meant to have any more children, but I didn't want to take any chances and was careful all of the time. There were some things that just couldn't be left to fate.

When the girls had both started school I started to think about getting a job. I'd enjoyed working before I was married. I'd liked having a job to go to and God knows that the extra money would come in handy, so I thought that it might be a good idea. Mick didn't see it that way.

'What do you want to get a job for?' he asked between the mouthfuls of food that he'd shovelled into his mouth.

'I just thought that it would be good.'

But Mick didn't agree, not just yet anyway – maybe when the girls were older.

I left it at that. For then. But I was determined that once Julie went to secondary school I was going to get a job. Or that was the plan until the day my world fell apart.

I discovered I was pregnant again. Mick was over the moon, the girls were excited, I was devastated. I didn't understand how it could have happened. Where had my plan gone wrong?

As Mick held his third daughter in his arms he looked as pleased as Punch. Even after eleven years of marriage I still didn't know if he loved me but I knew that he loved the girls. He loved them all, but as I watched him cradle his newest creation I knew that he would love this one the most.

Mick didn't mention it – why would he? It was women's stuff – but I think that he realised that, come what may, there would be no more children. His youngest daughter was all the more precious for that reason.

42

We decided to call her Susan. She was a good baby. She rarely cried and I have to admit that sometimes I used to forget she was there.

To an outsider looking in I was the perfect mother. My baby was always clean and looked content as she slept for hours at a time. People thought that I was the perfect wife too. Mick never went out without a clean shirt, there was always a crease in his trousers and his tea was always on the table when he got in from work. The girls were just the same; their dresses were always washed and ironed and they went to school every day.

Once, when Helen was about nine, I was at the gates waiting for the girls to come out of school when I saw Helen coming across the yard holding her teacher's hand. *What the hell has she done now?* I thought, and I knew that all the other mothers standing there were thinking the same.

'Mrs Thompson,' the teacher said, 'I wonder if I might have a word with you.' She was new to the school and I wasn't even sure what she was called. I'd never spoken to the woman before and from just the few words she'd said I could tell that she wasn't local.

'Is there something wrong?' I asked, trying to keep my voice down and hoping that she would do the same. But she didn't.

'I'm sure that you know that we have a spelling test every week, Mrs Thompson,' she said. 'I just wanted you to know that Helen is the only pupil that has got all of her spellings right every week this term. I wasn't sure if Helen would tell you herself and I thought that you should know. You should be very proud of her.'

I felt the eyes of the other mothers on me – and their disappointment that Helen wasn't in trouble. 'Well done, Helen love,' I said giving her a hug. I even gave her a kiss on the cheek. Later on I heard Helen tell Julie that, 'Mam hugged me.'

Mick was chuffed to bits when I told him. 'It's the grammar school for you,' he said as he ruffled her hair. 'That'll be a first for this family.'

She'd also be the first in the street, I thought. Now there would be something worth aiming for. It would really mean something if Helen could get into the grammar school. She would be special and, through her, the rest of us would be special too. The uniform would be a bit pricy but it'd be worth it to see the look on the faces of our neighbours. I could just imagine all the net curtains twitching as my daughter went past in her bottle-green uniform. Some of them might have to wipe the muck off their windows though, before they could see out of them.

That was one thing that you'd never hear me accused of. My house was always clean. The windows were washed inside and out every week, the beds were changed every week and I dusted and did the floors every day.

I once heard her, that one from the bottom of the street, saying that she didn't care what people thought about her. How could she not care what people thought about her? How could she not care what they said about the state of her curtains? People's opinions mattered. What they thought about you was everything. It didn't matter what was actually going on; you didn't let other people see your troubles. You could let them see the good stuff like your daughter in her grammar school uniform, but not the black eye that your husband had given you. Not that Mick ever gave me a black eye; he's never raised a finger to me in all the years I've known him, even though he could have a rotten temper. I might never have had a black eye, but if I'd had, no one would ever have seen it. Not the girls, not my mother and certainly not the neighbours.

But it turned out that Helen didn't get into grammar school. Julie didn't either, but then I'd never expected her to because she took after Mick's mother. All my hopes rested on Susan.

Helen did all right at school. I had hoped that she might have stopped on but she didn't want to know about it. After her exam results there probably wasn't much point anyway.

'You've got to think about your future,' I told her.

'I am,' she said, 'that's why I'm going to secretarial college.'

It was better than nothing I suppose.

There was a lad from the next street that stopped on. His mother was so proud. She mentioned it every time I saw her. She always made a point of asking how Helen was doing at college.

The trouble with Helen and college was the people she met. She might have been doing a secretarial course there but they taught other things at that college as well. Things like carpentry and mechanics. Helen started going out after college with her new friends. She said that there weren't any lads there but I know that there were. She must have thought that I was stupid. She was a sensible enough girl though. Julie was the one with an eye for the lads but she wasn't the type to get caught.

I didn't think that I'd have a problem with lads pestering Susan. Not unless things changed. Susan was a dumpy kid, not a bit like me or her sisters and her hair tended to be greasy which made it hang like rats' tails. She had pretty enough eyes but her face was a bit plain. I didn't see lads being a problem for her.

Even so she was Mick's favourite, just like I'd always known she would be.

I think Susan was about nine or ten when Mick's hours got cut at work. We were lucky that he didn't lose his job all together but it did leave us a bit short. Now I would have to get a job. Mick knew it as well as I did but he was worried about what would happen to his precious Susan.

'I've seen Pat next door,' I told him. 'She says that she'll bring Susan home and let her stay there playing with their Maggie until I get home. It'll only be for a couple of hours a day anyway.'

I don't think Mick was very happy about Susan being at a neighbour's house every day after school but we had no choice, we needed the money.

We needed it even more a few years later when Helen came home and said that she was getting married. She'd been going with Robert for a while but even so it was still a bit of a surprise. At least they'd booked the church ten months ahead so we had a bit of time to save up for it.

Less than a year after Helen's nuptials, Julie was getting married as well. It wasn't going to be the flash affair that Helen had had and I thanked God for that. Helen's reception had cost us a fortune. Julie said she wanted something more 'personal', which turned out to mean smaller, which suited me just fine. There was a bit of nonsense about the dress. Julie wanted an off-white dress – oyster or ivory or something she called it – but I soon put her straight. She'd get married in white and like it.

With two daughters safely married that just left Susan to worry about and, like I've said, I didn't think that would be a problem.

Helen made us grandparents in the June of the year after they were married. She had a baby boy and called him James Anthony. I tried to give Helen pointers about what she should do with the baby but I might as well have saved my breath for all the good it did. I loved being a grandma though; it fulfilled me in a way that being a mother never had.

\*\*\*

I looked at Susan one day and saw that she was growing up fast. She was a clever girl and doing all right at school. I even thought that she might go to university – well, hoped she would. She didn't seem that keen on the idea, but at least she planned on stopping on at school until she was eighteen, which was something.

She came home from school one day and said that one of the lasses in her class was going to a party and wanted her to go too. She wanted to know if she could go. I was touched by her asking because it was something that the other two had never done. I said that she could go, as long as she wasn't home too late. I was happy for her – I hadn't realised that she had any friends.

There were more parties after that one. It seemed like she was having a good time and that I hadn't been wrong about not having to worry about the lads chasing Susan. There was one boy eventually, but that didn't last very long. The ones that followed didn't last very long either and I didn't even meet most of them. But then she brought Tim home.

My heart sank when I saw them walking hand in hand. What the hell was she doing with him? Tim was Margaret and Billy Preston's youngest lad and he'd always been a tearaway.

But Susan wasn't having any of it. The more I told her that she could do better the less she listened. Then suddenly he decided that he was the one that could do better and he packed her in just before Christmas. My prayers had been answered. But then the nightmare began.

I think it was in the February that she was eighteen that I realised Susan had missed her period. Over the years I'd learned the tricks my own mam had used. It didn't matter how careful you were, there were always tell-tale signs that you were on your period. I'd always checked the girl's beds for signs that they were on but this time I searched without luck.

Oh my God! I felt sick at the thought that my suspicions might be right.

I faced Susan with my suspicions and gave her a pregnancy test to do. I breathed a sigh of relief when it was negative but when she still hadn't got her period a few days later I gave her a pot to pee in and told her to take it to the doctor's.

## SUSAN

Oh my God! Oh my God! Oh my God! The words just repeated themselves in my head as I sat facing the doctor. There had to be some mistake. I'd taken a test before and it had been negative. He had to be wrong. I hadn't come here for this. He had to be wrong.

'I'm very sorry, Susan,' the doctor said as he looked at me over those silly, half-moon glasses that sat on the end of his nose. I don't remember his name but I still remember the way he looked at me. He looked at me with sympathy – or was it pity? It was hard to tell. But that look ... there are some things the mind won't let you forget.

I just looked back at him and whispered, 'It's okay.'

Except it wasn't okay. It was anything but okay, but that wasn't his fault.

I must have walked out of the surgery but to be honest I don't remember doing it. I was in a daze and when I came to my senses I was sitting on the bench outside the doctor's watching the world go by. People were laughing. How could they be laughing? Looking back now it's easy to understand; their worlds weren't falling apart. It was just mine that was.

51

'What the hell am I going to do?' I asked myself the question over and over again. 'What the hell am I going to do?'

Have you ever had one of those moments when fate seems to intervene and something outside of you takes over? Well, I had one of those moments then. I turned to my right and saw the number 7 bus coming down the street. The number 7 stopped just around the corner from Julie's house. I had to see Julie. We hadn't been that close growing up but that had changed after Helen had left home. I often thought of what Julie had said to me on the night before she got married when she'd told me to be strong. I would need to be strong now and I would need Julie to help me.

The bus was coming and it was Wednesday. Julie never worked on Wednesdays so it was like someone was telling me to go there. So I did.

Julie had flour in her hair when she answered the door. 'Susan!' she seemed surprised to see me which I suppose was perfectly understandable. It wasn't as if I was a regular visitor to her house; I don't think I'd ever gone on my own before and certainly never unannounced. I burst out crying as I stood on her doorstep, my whole body shaking as I sobbed.

'Oh, come on, Susan,' she said putting her arm around me. 'What's the matter?'

I could only look at her because I didn't have the words that I needed.

'Come on in,' she said, and I let Julie lead me wherever she wanted to. She had to move me because it felt like I couldn't move myself. By the time I was sitting at the kitchen table my jacket was covered in the flour that had been on Julie's hands as well as in her hair. It was the least of my worries. As I sat at the table I was still crying but at least the sobbing had stopped.

Without me realising, Julie had made a pot of tea and she put a mug of it in front of me. I noticed that it was a flowery mug, a wedding present probably.

Julie didn't say anything for a long time and neither did I.

Eventually I said, 'I'm pregnant.'

Julie looked at me with her mug half way between her mouth and the table. Slowly she put it down.

'Pregnant?'

I nodded.

'Does she know?'

I didn't need to ask who the 'she' was that Julie was talking about. I shook my head. 'No, I only saw the doctor today.'

'What made you go to the doctor's?'

'She told me to go.'

53

'So she does know.'

'Not what he said, just that I was going.'

'Does she know what time you were going?'

I shrugged my shoulders. I honestly didn't know.

'Where does she think you are at the minute?'

'Don't know. Still at the doctor's I suppose.'

Julie took a deep breath and stretched her hands out across the table. I held them and now my hands were covered in flour too.

'Whose is it?'

'Tim's.'

'Preston's? Mum said you'd split up.'

'We have.' I was looking at the mug of tea on the table but I could feel Julie looking at me.

'How far along are you?'

I shrugged my shoulders. 'About eight weeks I think.'

We sat in silence, holding hands, for a long time.

After a while Julie squeezed my hands. 'I'd better ring her.'

'Why?' It was almost a scream.

'Because you don't need to make things any worse than they already are.'

How could they possibly be any worse? I didn't hear the telephone conversation but when she came back into the kitchen, Julie said, 'I told her that me and Chris will drop you off later.'

'What did she say?'

'Not a lot.'

'Did you tell her?'

'No love,' she said gently. 'That's down to you, I'm afraid.'

I started to cry again.

***

I don't think Chris asked why I was sitting at his kitchen table. He didn't ask why there was an unfilled pastry case sitting on the bench either. He didn't say anything when Julie told him that they would have to take me home, he just picked up his keys from where he had dropped them and went back out to the car,

Nobody said anything as we made the relatively short drive back to my parents' house and I was pleased about that. Julie sat in the back of the car with me and from time to time Chris would look at me through his rear-view mirror and smile. After he'd stopped the car we all sat for a second or two before Julie gave my arm a squeeze and said that we had to go in.

I looked at Chris in the mirror one last time. 'Don't worry,' he said, 'it'll be fine.'

I wished that I could have shared his optimism but I appreciated the sentiment and I tried to force a smile onto my face. I don't think I managed it.

'I'll not be long,' Julie told him but he told her to take as long as she needed.

Chris was a lovely bloke and Julie was very lucky.

Mum had her back to the kitchen door as we went in. I'm sure she heard us but she didn't turn around. Her shoulders heaved up and down as she washed pots in the sink and I could sense her anger. Eventually she turned her head and looked at us over her shoulder. Julie grabbed my hand and we stood by the door together.

'Wasn't expecting you, Julie,' Mum said. 'Chris not with you?'

'He's in the car.'

'Is he not coming in?'

'No.'

Mum snatched a tea towel from the drainer and dried her hands. She turned all the way round and the tension was painted all over her face. She tossed the towel aside and leaned back against the sink with her arms folded across her chest. Her mouth was twisted to one side and her eyes were cold,

'Well?' she said.

'Well what?' The words were out before I could stop them. It was a stupid thing to say and it just made her angrier, if such a thing was possible.

'Don't mess about with me, Susan,' she said sternly, 'What did the doctor say?'

I swear that was the moment that I felt my stomach hit the back of my throat.

'He said I'm pregnant,' I whispered and I felt Julie squeeze my hand even harder.

Mum let her head fall back so that she was looking up at the ceiling. Her chest heaved as she took deep breaths. It was like she was struggling to breathe and for a second I thought she was going to have a heart attack. Then she looked at me again.

'Your dad's in there.' She nodded towards the living room. 'You'd better go and tell him.'

'But...' I started to say.

'But nothing, lady,' she said, through gritted teeth. 'I said your dad's in there and you'd best go and tell him.'

***

Dad wasn't really watching the television. It was on but his head was half turned towards the kitchen like he had been listening to what had been going on in there. 'Susan?' he turned his head completely as I closed the door behind me.

57

'What's wrong Susan?' he asked as he turned the rest of his body in his chair to look at me.

Every part of me was trembling. I didn't know what to say or even where to start. In the end all I could do was take a deep breath and stammer out the words, 'I'm sorry Dad, but I'm pregnant.'

The look of disappointment on his face almost broke my heart. I couldn't stand to look at it because I knew I had let him down. 'I'm really sorry,' I said again and ran from the room. I ran up the stairs and into my bedroom closing the door behind me.

A few minutes later I heard a car start and I knew that Julie and Chris had left. I was alone with my parents and I didn't know what to expect next. I was scared beyond anything that I had felt before.

After a while I heard my parents talking in the kitchen which was directly below my bedroom. I could hear the voices but not what they were saying. I knew they would be talking about me though and I wanted – needed – to know what they were saying, so I carefully crept to the door and opened it a crack.

'I don't know why I'm getting the blame for this, Mick.' Mum said. Her voice was high, almost a screech and her words were crystal clear, but Dad's voice was lower and deeper and came across as a rumble so I couldn't make out what he was saying.

'Yeah well it's not my fault.' There was a pause and the next time I heard Mum her voice wasn't quite so high-pitched. 'I just don't believe it. Julie I could have understood, but not Susan. I'd never thought that this would have happened to Susan.'

Why not me I thought? What was wrong with me?

'It's a bloody mess, that's all I know,' I heard Dad say. They must have moved into the living room because now I could hear both sides of the conversation. 'He'll have to marry her,' Dad said and the thought of me being married to Tim Preston made me feel cold all over. I screamed one word in my head: *No!*

'Over my dead body,' Mum said, and for once we were in agreement.

'Well what else can we do? The lad should face up to his responsibilities.'

'I don't know much,' Mum said, 'but I know that I'll not have a Preston in this family.'

'Bit late for that, Jean,' Dad said. 'We've already got a Preston in the family and she's carrying it in her belly.'

I thought I was going to throw up.

'What about your Aunty Rose?' Mum asked.

59

'What about her?'

'We could send Susan to live with her in Scarborough until the baby's born. She could put the baby up for adoption and come back afterwards and no one will ever know.'

'Are you mad woman?' Dad said. 'My Aunty Rose is ninety-four for a start and even if she did go where are we supposed to say that she's been?'

'Scarborough.'

'For nine months? Some bloody holiday that is. No, we can't do that.'

'Well I don't know what else we can do.'

Apparently my dad didn't know either because all I could hear was silence from below.

I sat on the floor with my knees pulled up to my chin and thought about the mess that I'd got myself into.

As I thought about what Mum had said, I felt sick. Not the bit about Dad's Aunty Rose, I wouldn't have minded spending some time with her. We hadn't seen her for years but she had always been nice to me. But she was far too old to be involved in what Mum was planning. *I* didn't even want to be involved in what Mum was planning, especially not the part about giving the baby up for adoption. Like it or not, I was having a baby and it was part of me. It was part of them too, yet here she was talking about me giving it to a

60

complete stranger. How could she do that? I couldn't imagine how I would be able to give it away; I would constantly be looking over my shoulder every time I passed a child that was the same age and sex wondering if it was mine. No, I couldn't give it away, I just couldn't. Somehow I was going to have to convince Mum that was a bad idea.

Eventually I made my way back to my bed and lay down. I felt drained. I turned onto my side and pulled my knees up to my chest. Wasn't this what they called the foetal position? Is this how my baby was lying in my womb?

My baby. My baby. My baby. I emphasised each word in my head. A baby was a helpless thing, something that had to be looked after, and this was my baby so I was the one that was going to have to look after it.

The next morning I didn't know what sort of reception to expect. I hadn't seen my parents since I'd told Dad about the baby. I hadn't left my bedroom and no one had come up to see how I was. I didn't mind so much because I'd wanted to be alone but I couldn't stay there forever.

I'd heard Dad leave for work an hour or so earlier just like he always did and I'd lain in bed since then and listened to Mum moving around downstairs. I waited for her to shout me down for breakfast, but she didn't. I looked at the clock

61

on the bedside table and waited, but still the call didn't come. Eventually I got up and started to get ready for school.

I came out of the bathroom after having a wash to find my mother waiting for me. She had a basket of ironing in her hands

'You're up then,' she stated the obvious.

I nodded my head and avoided eye contact as I squeezed past her. 'I need to get ready for school,' I said quietly.

'School? I don't think so, lady,' she said.

'But I've got to,' I said. 'I missed yesterday.'

'Yeah, well you'll be missing another one today. I'll ring and tell them you're not very well.' She pushed towels into a cupboard and slammed the door.

'Are you going to tell them?' I asked nervously.

'Are you stupid?' she hissed. 'Of course I'm not going to bloody tell them.'

'But what about my exams?'

'What about them? You can kiss goodbye to them.'

'Why? Carol Malone was pregnant and she still did her exams.'

'I don't care what Carol Malone did.' She folded towels as she talked. 'You're not going to school pregnant. They're not even going to know that you're pregnant.' She spat the word out every time she said it. 'You remember your dad's Aunty Rose in Scarborough...?'

'But she's old.'

'Is she now?' Mum stopped folding the towels and stared at me. 'Well her daughter's not and she's the one that you'll be staying with. Your dad rang his cousin Sally last night and she's agreed to have you. Your dad's going to take you over on Sunday. You can stay with her until the baby's born and that'll give us time to sort out an adoption.'

'Adoption!' Even though I'd known what she was thinking I still couldn't believe that she was really suggesting it to me.

'Yes, adoption.' Mum started folding clothes again. 'What did you think you were going to do?'

'Keep it.'

'Keep it?' She made a noise that was a mix between a snort and a laugh. 'And have your life ruined?'

'Why would it be ruined?'

She sighed heavily. 'Because it would.'

That didn't seem like much of an explanation to me.

'What about Tim?' I almost didn't dare to ask the question.

'It's got nothing to do with him.'

'It's his baby.'

'He didn't want you, Susan,' she said callously, 'so what makes you think that he'd want you and your baby?'

That hurt so much. 'But he has a right to know.'

The look in Mum's eyes told me that she didn't agree with me.

Thank God she couldn't bring herself to look at me for very long because I couldn't stand the look on her face. All I had ever wanted to do in my life was please Mum enough for her to love me and now that was never going to happen. I had brought the ultimate shame on the family and I knew that she would never forgive me.

## JEAN

I knew there was something wrong as soon as Susan wasn't home by four o'clock.

I'd nearly gone to the doctor's with her but that would have set tongues wagging. There'd be bound to be someone in the surgery who knew us and it would be bad enough when they saw Susan go in alone – you know, wondering what was wrong with her – but if the two of us were there that'd be it; we'd be the talk of the place. I mean, Susan wasn't a kid any more; she didn't need to be taken to the doctor's. Me being there with her would scream pregnancy test. In the end I'd had to let her go on her own while I stayed at home to get on with what needed doing. Not that I could concentrate, I just went through the motions really, working on auto-pilot and looking at the clock every five minutes.

After a bit I turned the pan of potatoes off and went to the kitchen window to watch for her coming. The doctor's surgery was only a ten-minute walk away and I was sure that she'd said her appointment was early afternoon.

I thought about going along to see if she was there, but how would that look? Then I thought about ringing the surgery to check what time her appointment had been but there was no point because they wouldn't tell me anything. Anyway, that snotty cow from number thirty-six worked on the reception and I didn't like talking to her at the best of times. The more I thought about it, the more I thought that Susan had said her appointment was early afternoon. Something about half past two rang a bell.

It could mean only one thing. She would have been straight home if the test had been negative. She'd have wanted to prove me wrong. There could only be one explanation and it made me feel sick.

Oh my God, not her; not this. My mind went back to the day that I'd found out I was having Helen, the day my mam had sent me to meet Mick out of work so that I could tell him. I had been terrified that day and I had cried all the way to the factory gates. Back in those days when a lass fell wrong there was nothing to be done but marry the lad and be grateful that he didn't desert you. Had things changed any? They had if you believed what you read in the papers, and maybe they had in some other places, but not round here. I'd seen the way people looked at girls with a baby and no man. I knew that look because I'd looked at them that way myself.

66

I didn't want people looking at Susan that way but I didn't want her going down the same road that I had either.

I prayed to God that she hadn't gone to tell that Preston lad, Tim or whatever he was called. I'd known he'd be trouble. The whole flaming family were trouble and I couldn't stand the thought of one of my daughters being stuck with one of them for the rest of her life.

I mean, was he even going to want her? They'd fallen out a few weeks earlier and I'd seen him just a couple of days ago outside his grandma's house snogging on with one of Eileen Jones' lasses. He wasn't going to want Susan – not now, not just because she was in trouble. God knows if anyone else would want her now either. Who the hell would choose to take on another man's baby?

I was relieved when Julie rang to say that Susan was with her because at least it meant she hadn't gone to him. I didn't bother asking why Susan was there, I didn't need to. There was nothing to do but get on with tea and wait for all hell to break loose.

I was crying as I put the mashed potatoes on top of the shepherd's pie and when it was in the oven I sat at the table with my head in my hands and wondered what on earth I was going to tell Mick. I couldn't do it. I couldn't be the one to tell him that his precious Susan was no better than her mother. It would break his heart and I wasn't about to do that. We might not have had a marriage made in Heaven but I thought a lot of him and I didn't like to see him hurt.

But never mind what was I going to tell Mick, what was I going to tell the neighbours? Her at the bottom of the street would have a field day. She'd had to take all the gossip when her youngest had had a baby the year before and she be quick to get her own back. Why hadn't I kept my mouth shut?

When I heard the van pull up outside and drop Mick off I grabbed a tissue and dried my eyes. He walked through the door and did a double take when he looked at me. He couldn't help but see that I'd been crying but he didn't say anything. He did ask where Susan was though.

'Library,' I said, saying the first thing that came into my head.

He looked surprised but didn't say anything, he just sat at the table and waited for his tea to be dished up. I put a plate of food in front of both of us but I couldn't face mine. I pushed the plate away and sat back in my chair.

'What's wrong with your tea?' he asked as he shovelled another forkful into his mouth.

'Nothing,' I said, 'I just don't feel like it.'

'That's not like you,' he said. 'You only go off your food when you're pregnant. Not got something to tell me have you?' he laughed.

Oh God, if only he knew.

After he had finished his tea, Mick took the paper out of the pocket of the coat he'd hung on the back of his chair and disappeared into the living room just like he did every night. I set about washing the dishes, looked at the clock every two minutes and waited for Susan.

When she did eventually come home, Julie was by her side.

I was washing a saucepan when she came through the door and I kept my hands in the water for a few seconds before I turned round, grabbed a tea towel and dried them. She looked pathetic and I didn't need to ask her what the doctor had said because it was written all over her face. I did though, because until I heard her say the words there was still hope.

I told her straight that she was going to have to tell her dad herself. She wasn't keen on that at first, she was all tears and 'buts', but I wasn't having any of it. 'He's in there,' I said, nodding towards the living room and, to be fair to her, she went off without another word.

'Be kind to her Mam,' Julie said.

'Kind to her! What do you mean be kind to her?'

'You know, not too hard on her. She's just a kid.'

'Who's having her own kid.'

'Yeah, and she's not the first and she'll certainly not be the last.'

Julie had always been a bit headstrong, but she had never been openly defiant towards me before.

'Your husband's waiting,' I said.

She gave me a look that I'd never seen before but she didn't say anything else. She went to the back door and opened it. Before she left, she told me to tell Susan to ring her if she needed her. I wondered what Julie had told Chris.

I leaned against the sink and waited for what would happen next. After a few minutes I heard the door to the hall slam shut and the sound of footsteps on the stairs. She'd told him then. I stood where I was and waited.

I had to wait for what seemed like a long time and I wondered what was happening in the living room. I'd expected Mick to come into the kitchen but there was no sign of him and the only sound was the television. The news had ended and I could hear the theme tune of a soap opera that Mick hated. He always turned the channel over before it came on, but not tonight. For a second I thought he might have had a heart attack and I wondered if I should go in and check on him, but I was afraid of what I might find so I waited a bit longer.

Eventually he did come into the kitchen. He had aged ten years in as many minutes. He shook his head. 'Is she sure?' he asked.

'Yes,' I said. 'She saw the doctor this afternoon.'

'He might be wrong.'

'He's not wrong, Mick,' I said. Well there was no point giving him false hope. 'She's pregnant all right.'

He looked at me and I didn't like what I saw. 'You knew didn't you,' he said and although it wasn't a physical shout it felt like one. It was certainly an accusation.

'No.'

'Yes you did,' he said angrily. Mick hadn't been angry in years, God he hadn't been anything in years. 'Yes you did,' he said again, 'there's nothing that goes on in this house that you don't know about. You knew and you didn't tell me.'

'What was I supposed to say,' I said, feeling like I had to defend myself. 'I thought that she might be but I hoped that I was wrong. She'd done a home test and that had been negative.'

'So this one might be wrong.' The sound of him grasping at straws was pitiful.

'Oh stop it, Mick,' I snapped. 'Of course it's not wrong.'

71

We stood and looked at each other. We hadn't argued in years and it was like neither of us knew what to do next.

'How did you let this happen?'

What did he mean how did *I* let this happen? I hadn't let anything happen and I told him as much and stormed past him into the living room. By the time I'd turned the television off and turned around he was behind me. I think I said something about how I wouldn't have been surprised if it had happened to Julie, but not Susan; I just couldn't believe that Susan could have been that stupid.

I nearly died when Mick suggested that the Preston lad would have to marry her. What the hell was he thinking? I knew what it was, of course; he was thinking that he'd had to accept the responsibility for what had happened all those years ago, had to deal with the consequences, and if he'd had to why should this lad not have to do the same? Because he was a Preston that was why and I wasn't having one in the family. Mick thought he was being clever by saying something about there already being a Preston in the family and I wanted to smack him across the face. I didn't know how he could joke at a time like this. But he wasn't really joking, was he? He was just stating the bloody obvious.

Mick went mad when I suggested that we send Susan to stay with his Aunt Rose. 'She's ninety-four,' he said. I was very well aware of how old she was but why would that matter? She might enjoy having Susan stop for a while. Rose had always got on well with her when we used to take the girls to Scarborough on holiday. She used to feed her custard creams every chance she got.

I watched Mick pace up and down the room. He was muttering something that I couldn't hear and his eyes were flitting from one side to the other. He reminded me of a bear that we'd seen in a zoo that we'd taken the girls to one summer; it was in a cage that anyone could see was way too small for it and it looked like it was going out of its mind. Mick had that same look on his face.

His pacing took him to an armchair and he turned around and dropped into it. On any other day I'd have played merry hell with him because that's how the seats got damaged but that day wasn't a day for worrying about furniture. Mick rested his elbows on his knees and held his head in his hands.

I lowered myself carefully into the chair opposite him. 'I don't know what to do,' I said, admitting defeat – and trust me, that wasn't a good feeling. I might have thought Rose was a possibility but, well, I knew it wasn't really; if for no other reason than that, at her age Rose could pass away at any minute and then Susan would have to come home and we'd have a hell of a job hiding our shame then.

What were we going to do? What were we going to do?

And then it came to me.

'Sally,' I said.

'What?' or at least I think that's what Mick grunted.

'Sally,' I said. 'She could go and stay with Sally.' He sat up straight so I thought that I had grabbed his attention. 'Think about it Mick. Sally's granddaughter was eight months old before we even knew she existed.'

'So?'

'So, she'd be sympathetic. She's been where we are right now.'

He wasn't very keen but eventually he agreed to give Sally a ring. I wasn't any happier than he was about Susan going to stay with her but I didn't know what else to do. She had to go somewhere.

I watched Mick dial the number and wait for the phone to be answered at the other end. After the usual pleasantries were out of the way Mick got to the point.

'We need a favour Sally,' he said and waited for her reply. 'Susan's got herself into a bit of trouble and we were wondering if she could come and stay with you for a while.' He nodded his head as he listened to what Sally was saying.

They chatted for a couple of minutes and then he said, 'Thank you Sally, I'll bring her over at the weekend.'

'She'll take her,' Mick said after he put the phone down. 'I've said I'll take her at the weekend.'

I didn't say anything, had he forgotten that I'd been sitting beside him?

'Do you think we should have asked Susan first though?'

'She'll do as she's told,' I said. 'We're her parents and she'll do as she's told. We only want what's best for her, she'll see that.' I'm not sure he believed what I was saying any more than I did. 'I'll go and tell her,' I said, as I got out of the chair.

'No,' he said, 'leave her be tonight.'

It could keep until the morning.


Mick didn't say a word to me the following morning. He was up and in the bathroom before I'd even turned the alarm off and he got dressed while I made his sandwiches. He'd put his coat on and grabbed his sandwiches before he even looked at me. 'Tell Susan that Sally is just an option,' he said. 'She doesn't have to go if she doesn't want to.'

Did she not? Well we'd see about that.

After he'd gone I made a cup of tea and sat at the table. I stared at the tea until it was cold. I knew that I couldn't eat, but I'd thought that a drink might do me good. But when push came to shove I couldn't bear the thought of putting anything in my mouth.

There was so much to do before Sunday so I tried to put my thoughts into some sort of order. I had to regain control. There was no point buying her maternity clothes because who knew what sort of size she'd be? We'd have to give Sally some money for clothes and other things that she was going to need. That, on top of what we were going to have to give Sally for Susan's keep, was going to wipe out all of the money that we had in the bank but it had to be done and I was already resigned to having no holiday that year even though we had been talking of maybe going on one of those package holidays that were always being advertised.

Susan was late getting up. I looked at the clock and wondered where she was. She didn't have an alarm because she didn't need one. She woke up at the same time every day, but it looked like her internal clock had failed her for once in her life because she was late. I decided to let her rest; there was no rush for her to get up. There'd be no school today so there was nothing to get up for.

Almost an hour later than normal, I heard her in the bathroom. I was walking up the stairs with a basket full of ironing that I'd done the day before when I heard the water running. I was stacking the towels when she came out of the bathroom.

Oh my God she looked terrible. I asked her what she was doing and, bless her, in all innocence she said that she was going to school. What the hell was the girl thinking? She seemed surprised when I said that there'd be no school for her that day, and even more so when I said that there'd be no more school for her full stop.

'What about my exams?' she said.

What about her bloody exams? She couldn't do them this year, but if she listened to me and did what I said maybe she'd be able to do them next year when she came back. Things like her exams were exactly the reason why I wanted her to have the baby adopted. Well, that and the fact that I didn't want one of my girls to be marked as an unmarried mother. I know people would probably laugh at me but I didn't want her to feel the shame that I had.

Anyway she was going on about her exams and was saying that some girl at school had had a baby and managed to do hers. Well that's as may be but it wasn't going to happen to her. And that was when I told her what *was* going to happen to her.

'Do you remember your dad's aunt Rose?' I asked and she said that she did. She also said that Rose was old. 'Yes,

77

well, she might be,' I said, 'but Sally's not. Your dad rang her last night and you are going to stay with her. That'll give us some time to organise an adoption.'

'What do you mean adoption?'

'You can't keep the baby, Susan.'

'Why not?'

Why not? Was she having a laugh? That was the first time that I'd said the word adoption out loud. I'd assumed that Mick understood that was the plan but I didn't think that Susan would get it. I know Mick had said to tell her that it was just an option but I didn't. It wasn't an option as far as I was concerned, so what was the point? She just needed to get her head around preparing herself to give the baby away. If she thought there was a chance she might keep it, she would start to get attached to it and that wouldn't be good for anyone, least of all Susan. No, just let her think that adoption was the only way.

She obviously thought that there *were* other options and she mentioned Tim again.

'I should tell Tim,' she said. 'If I tell Tim he might help me.'

Help her? He'd helped himself to what he had wanted and then he'd been off like a shot. I hated myself afterwards for saying it, but it was out before I could stop it.

'Susan,' I said, 'he didn't want you before, so he's not going to want you just because you're having a baby.'

Her eyes could hardly contain the tears that were forming. 'Maybe,' she said, 'but he has a right to know.'

I didn't say anything, mainly because I was afraid of what I might say. I just looked at her for a second or two. It was all I could manage.

## SUSAN

I watched Mum walk down the stairs and wondered how she could be so cruel. It wasn't so much what she had said about Tim not wanting me, though God knows that was bad enough, it was the adoption thing. How could she expect me to give up my baby? I'd had all night to think about it and I still couldn't see how I could ever do such a thing. I'm not criticising people that do have their babies adopted; I just knew that it wasn't for me. This was my doing and I was prepared to take responsibility for it. Plus, the thing was – and I know this might sound stupid because at that point my baby was no more than a tiny bunch of cells – I loved it. I'd thought, hoped, that Mum might have reconsidered over night, but obviously not.

I made my way back to my bedroom, closed the door behind me and looked at the teddy bear that was sitting at the bottom of my bed. I grabbed hold of it, clutched it to my chest and flopped down on the bed. I lay on my back and looked at the ceiling. I needed her, really needed her, and she was more concerned with what the neighbours would think; I knew that was at the bottom of the adoption plan. For as long as I could remember Mum had created this façade of being the perfect housewife and mother, and me with a bump would shatter that illusion.

To be fair to her, in Mum's mind hiding me away until it was all over and then getting rid of the evidence was probably the only way out of this that she could even see. For once, though, she wasn't going to get her own way. I had to do something. I couldn't let what Mum was planning happen. Last night I'd realised that I was the one that had to look after my baby but, more than that, I *wanted* to look after my baby and I was going to. Mum might not be going to look after her child, but I was going to look after mine.

From now on, it was just me and my baby. As I lay there on the bed a plan started to form in my head.

\*\*\*

'We'll not be long,' Mum said.

'It's all right,' I told her without taking my eyes off the television. I tried to appear uninterested. She said something about my dad needing a couple of pints after a hard day at work. I didn't care why they needed to go, just that they did, and all the while that they were getting ready my mind was ticking over with what I had to do.

81

Mum was already in the kitchen when Dad came downstairs and I was surprised when I saw him appear in the living room.

'What you watching?' he asked.

It didn't matter that I couldn't really explain what I was watching because he didn't really want to know. It was as if he'd just come into the room to see me. I thought he was going to say something else but he didn't, well, not unless you count, 'See you later.'

I let out a sigh of relief when they were finally out of the house. It was time. My legs shook as I climbed the stairs. They had both told me that they wouldn't be long so I worked out that the walk there and back was ten minutes each way, which with, say, an hour for a couple of pints, should give me at least an hour and a half.

It wasn't a lot of time.

I hadn't dared risk packing my bag before, out of fear that Mum might find it, so now was the time to do it and do it quickly. Okay, so think. I crawled under the bed and grabbed the holdall that Mum had bought me when I'd gone away with the school the year before. It was covered in dust, so I bashed it, and coughed as the dust flew everywhere.

What would I need? I had no idea so I threw some underwear in the bag along with a pair of shoes, some T-

82

shirts and a couple of pairs of jeans. I opened the drawer and fumbled through it until I found my bank book. There wasn't a lot in it but there'd be enough for a bus ticket to where I needed to go, or at least I hoped that there would be. Would there be enough for a taxi to the bus station? Probably not and anyway I was going to have to be careful with the little money that I did have.

Did I mention where I was going? Sorry, I should have said this before. Just after the doctor had told me that I was pregnant he'd handed me a leaflet which I hadn't paid much attention to at the time. I'd shoved it into my pocket, not thinking that I would need it. How wrong had I been? When I'd realised that it was me and my baby against the world, I had got the leaflet out my pocket and read it.

'Are you pregnant and in crisis?' it said in big, bold letters cross the top and there was a telephone number underneath. 'Call anytime,' it said, 'day or night. So that's what I had done. Mum had sent me to town the day before to buy a couple of things that I would need for Scarborough and I had taken the opportunity to use a pay phone to ring them.

I remember my hands shaking as I rang the number and feeling my teeth chatter against each other as I waited for someone to pick up. I was so nervous. I could hardly believe

83

that I was actually doing it. After three or four rings a woman's voice introduced herself as Sharon and asked how she could help.

'Hello,' I said, my voice shaking as much as my hands had been, 'I'm pregnant and in crisis.' I'll never forget those words.

'Then you've called the right place,' Sharon had said and asked me what my name was.

I told her.

'All right, Susan,' her voice was calm and reassuring. She'd asked me if I was in danger and I told her all about my mum wanting to send me away and how she wanted me to give my baby away. 'And is that not what you want, Susan?'

No, it most certainly wasn't what I wanted.

She said that she could help me and a wave of relief flooded over me. She asked me where I lived and when I told her she asked if I realised that they were about forty miles away. I said that I did. I remembered what the doctor had said to me. He had said that they weren't local and before that moment I hadn't really thought about what 'not local' meant. Apparently it meant forty miles away.

'Can you get to us, Susan?' she asked.

'Yes,' I said without thinking.

'Then we'll be waiting for you,' she said.

So that was my plan. I was going to a refuge for girls like me. When I'd first come up with the idea, I could hardly believe that I was planning on running away from home but here I was getting ready to go. Sharon had given me exact instructions on how to get to the house and I read through them again. *Stop it*, I said to myself, *stop putting it off. Go now. Go now while you can. You don't have time to waste.*

I put my jacket on, checked that I had the leaflet and the instructions safely stowed in my pocket and that my purse and bank book were in my holdall. I left my bedroom without a backward glance, closed the door behind me and trotted down the stairs. I plucked my house key from the window sill and used it to lock the door behind me. As soon as that was done I posted the key back through the letter box.

I made my way down the path to the gate. I had to open it carefully because the hinge needed oiling and usually squeaked. I was scared that in the silence of the darkness the squeak would be louder than it normally was and I didn't want to attract any attention. I was surprised when the gate opened silently. Were the god's looking out for me?

On the other side of the gate I did allow myself a look back at the house, just for a second. It was the only home that I had ever known and here I was leaving it without a word to anyone. I forced myself to move. I had to get to the bus station.

I took the round about way into town. The quickest route would have taken me past the pub that was my parents' local and I didn't want to take the chance of them being by a window and looking out just at the wrong moment. So it was the back streets for me and I didn't see anyone apart from an old woman who seemed drunk, or doolally, it was hard to tell.

'You all right love?' she asked as she hung on to a wall. 'Where are you going with that bag?'

'Nowhere,' I said and rushed past her.

Once I was in the town centre there weren't too many people about and none of them were interested in me. They were more interested in which pub they were going to go into next. I made my way to the bus station as quickly as I could.

Once there I searched out the board and looked at the timetable for the number 84 that would take me to where I needed to go. I was disappointed to find that there were no more buses that night. The last one had left just after seven o'clock. According to the timetable, the next one was at six-thirty-six the next morning, would take an hour and a half and cost me £5. That was just about half the cash that I had so I would have to get some more.

Every second of that night is still clear in my head and when I think about it I'm seeing it just as I did then; it's as if I'm there all over again and right at that second when I realised I needed more money I was scared because it occurred to me that I didn't know what I would do if I couldn't get any. I needed the money to get away.

I looked around, trying to get my bearings, and realised there was a branch of my bank nearby. Luckily for me, it had a cashpoint outside it. I had only used the machine once before and I hoped that I could remember my PIN number. When I got to the machine there was already someone using it, so I held back and waited until they had moved away. Making sure that there was no one else around I approached the machine and put my card in. I was careful to put the numbers in in what I thought was the right order and pressed the buttons to take all but £2.34 out of my account. Three £10 notes popped out of the machine and I folded them carefully and put them into the toe of one of the shoes in the bottom of my holdall. I looked around to make sure that no one had seen me but I was the only person left on the street, apart from someone throwing up in a flower bed.

Then it started to rain. Great big, heavy drops that went from nothing to a torrent in a matter of moments and within seconds my hair was flat against my head and my jacket felt heavy on my shoulders. There was a café in the bus station and I ran there as quickly as I could. I would be able to shelter there while I thought of what I was going to do next. I wasn't the only person to have had this idea and I found myself in a queue of four or five people.

'Coffee please,' I said when it was my turn to be served.

'Big or small?' the surly woman behind the counter asked.

'Big, please,' I said. I know it was a bit of an extravagance but, under the circumstances, I thought I deserved it. Plus, judging by the amount of rain that was falling, it didn't look like I'd be going anywhere any time soon.

I handed over the right change and thanked the woman. She looked surprised but given her surly outlook she probably didn't see a lot of gratitude for her customer service skills. Mum had brought me up to be polite though and I always thanked people when they did something for me, regardless of how they did it.

I took the coffee and moved away from the counter. There were about a dozen people sitting at various tables and

I made my way to an empty one at the back that was furthest away from the door and closest to the toilet.

I don't know if I can describe how I felt right then. It's not that I can't remember because, as I think about it now, the feelings are as real as they were that night. I just don't have the vocabulary to describe it. I was more than sad. I mean, what did I have to be happy about? I was pregnant by a boy who had dumped me as soon as a better offer had come along, my mother was so ashamed of me that she wanted to send me away until I'd had a baby that she then wanted me to give away and I had run away from home. Life was just peachy.

But though I was sad, I wasn't despondent, if that makes sense. In an odd sort of way I was feeling positive. For the first time in my life I had got the courage from somewhere to stand up to my mother, and I was doing something to protect the life that I had created. When it had been important enough, I had finally found the strength to do something I'd never done before. Whether Mum liked it or not I was going to have a baby and, more than that, I had no intention of giving it up. I didn't know what the future would hold, I didn't even know what was going to happen in the next twenty-four hours, but I was *doing* something and that made me feel good inside.

I'd been sitting at the table a while sipping my coffee, trying to make it last as long as possible, when I felt someone looking at me. You know the feeling, when you can just sense that you are being watched. I looked around the café and found that there were a few more people at the tables than there had been when I'd first come in, but none of them were looking at me. Most were staring into their cups, one was reading a paper, and I think that a couple of others might have been asleep.

But then I saw him. My dad was at the window looking at me as I looked at him. So, my secret was out and they were looking for me. Well, he was looking for me – there was no sign of my mum. I fully expected him to walk in and drag me home. Maybe not drag, because that wasn't Dad's style, but you know what I mean. But he didn't. He just stood in the pouring rain looking at me as I looked at him.

Eventually he lifted his hand to his mouth and rested the tips of his fingers to his lips. Then he put those fingertips on the window and without thinking, or even realising at the time that I was doing it, I lifted my own hand up and caught the kiss that he had thrown me.

Through tears, I watched my dad turn away from the window and walk away.

I remember seeing the now lukewarm coffee wobble in the cup as I tried to lift it with shaking hands. I put the cup down and held my hands together. Dad had blown me a kiss and walked away. Why would he do that? Mum must have told him to bring me home when he found me, so why hadn't he? I wasn't imagining it, he had seen me and that kiss was like thousands of other kisses that he had thrown me before. It was like he had seen me and, without actually speaking the words, had given me his blessing for what I was doing. It was as though he was telling me to get away while I could. It was the closest thing to Dad standing up to Mum that I had ever seen. Part of me wanted to chase after him and go home. I loved my dad dearly and I knew he loved me back. I couldn't bear the thought of Mum giving him a hard time when he got home without me. But wasn't that what he wanted? He clearly wanted me to go through with whatever it was I was doing and I wasn't going to let him down. He didn't know what my plan was but he trusted me enough to carry it out.

I had a renewed strength and I was more determined than ever.

'Right you lot,' the surly assistant said, 'we're closing in ten minutes, so finish your drinks and make yourself scarce.'

For the first time that day I found myself smiling. With charm like that, the woman could have worked in the best of establishments, yet here she was working in a greasy café in a deserted bus station in the middle of the night. Amazing.

The few people that were left started to leave so I quickly drank what was left of the almost cold coffee and started to make my own way out of there. I picked up my holdall and swung it over my shoulder leaving my hands free to pick up my mug and carry it to the counter.

'Thank you,' I said as I put it down.

'You're welcome, love,' she said kindly. She surprised me when she added, 'You look after yourself.'

She held me with her eyes for a second and then she surprised me again by smiling at me. I smiled back.

I was the last customer to leave and she followed me to the door. I heard her lock it behind me and I could feel her watching me as I walked away.

I started to walk, though I wasn't sure where I was going. I didn't know where to go. I had six and a half hours of rainy night to kill and I had no idea how I was going to do it.

And then I saw it, the steeple of St Mary's church peeping over the top of the dress shop in front of me, lit up like a beacon. Luckily for me this was back in the days when churches were left open twenty-four hours a day, offering a safe haven for the helpless and the needy. God knows that I fell into at least one of those categories, so I made my way there.

But when I got to the door it wouldn't open and I wondered if I'd been wrong about the safe haven thing. I turned the handle again and pushed a little harder, it seemed to give a bit so I pushed my shoulder against it and the door opened with a creak. Once inside I closed the door carefully behind me, forcing it back into place. Without thinking I dipped my fingers into the font of water by the door and blessed myself.

There was a faint glow lighting the church which I soon realised was from the candles that were alight in front of various statues. I felt myself drawn to the statue at the front of the church perhaps because she was lit up the brightest on account of all the candle spaces in front of her being taken. All except one that was.

I dropped my bag to the floor and dug into my pocket for my purse. I rummaged around for some coins which I dropped into the tin before picking up a candle from the basket in front of me. I touched the candle on my forehead, my chest, both shoulders and finally my lips before I lit it from one of the candles that was already there and secured it into the last place on the stand. I knelt before the statue of

Our Lady and prayed. I'm not sure how long I knelt there but it wasn't as if there was a queue so I prayed until I was ready to stop by which time I felt more at ease with myself.

I stood up and looked at the statue one last time before starting to walk around the church that I'd been in hundreds of times. I'd never been in at night before and to see it in candlelight left me amazed by how beautiful it was. Before it had just been a church but now it felt like so much more. It really was my haven.

There were four or five other people taking refuge in the church that night: a couple of old men who looked like they were wearing every piece of clothing they owned and were badly in need of a bath and, a few pews back, a well-dressed woman who reeked of booze and was fast asleep, leaning back in the pew that she was sitting in. Further back still was a younger woman who was drawing something, the altar I think, and there might have been someone else in the section of the church that wasn't lit, but I wasn't really sure.

I selected the pew opposite the younger woman, the one that was drawing. There was a wall at the end of the pew and I settled against it using my holdall as a pillow.

I was almost scared to go to sleep – I had a bus to catch – I didn't want to miss it but I was so tired I felt my eyes closing. I fought it for a while, then gave in to the sleep that I badly needed. It was a fitful sleep, more like a series of dozes really, and the sound of the priest preparing for the six o'clock mass woke me up completely. Through half-open eyes I watched him for a few minutes as he laid a cloth here and placed a chalice there. I forced my eyes fully open and saw that I was the only one of the night visitors left. When the priest retired to the sacristy I made my escape, being careful to genuflect to the altar again and bless myself on the way out. Old habits die hard. As I walked away from the church I saw a couple of people who looked as though they were making their way to the early morning mass but apart from them the streets were deserted.

When I got to the bus station, the clock above it read 6.15am so I made my way to the right stand and was about to join the queue of people waiting for the number 84 when I had a thought. Julie. I couldn't leave without a word to Julie. I couldn't ring her; I didn't trust myself not to say more than I should. I knew I had a stamp in my purse so I could send her a letter if only I had some paper. I looked around and saw that the newsagent in the corner of the station was open. I went in and bought a writing pad, a pen and some envelopes before joining the bus queue, which had six people in it.

The bus doors had just opened and the first of the passengers was climbing aboard. I waited my turn and then did the same. 'Single please.' I said to the driver who paid me no attention as he produced a ticket and gave me my change.

There were two people sitting in the lower deck of the bus. They were both at the back so I took a seat just behind the driver. I had just opened the carrier bag of goodies that I had bought from the newsagent and looked inside when it occurred to me that I was going to need to post my letter before the bus left. If I didn't, it would bear the postmark of the town I was going to and I didn't want anyone – not even Julie – to know where that was. There was a post box in the station, I could see it from where I was sitting, but I would need to be quick.

I pulled the pad out, used my teeth to get the top off the pen and wrote the words quickly. I can't remember what those words were exactly but it was something along the lines of thank you for everything you did for me and that I was sorry to leave without saying goodbye but that I had to keep my baby safe and that meant leaving without anyone knowing where I was going. I ended by telling her not to worry and that I would be all right. The writing was really bad and I hoped that Julie would be able to read it. I had no time to do it again so I would have to take the chance.

I quickly folded the paper and put it into one of the envelopes. I wrote the address as quickly as I could and stuck a stamp in the corner.

I stood up, leaving my bag on my seat and approached the driver. 'I just need to post this letter,' I said, 'I'll be back in a minute.'

'You'd better be,' he said, 'because we leave in two,' and I heard him start the engine.

As it happened I was back in plenty of time and the bus was still sitting there a good three or four minutes after I'd got back on. After loading one last passenger who had come running up to the bus, the driver closed the door and we were off.

'Thought I wasn't going to make it,' the late-comer said. He was a man of about my dad's age and looked like he was dressed for work. He had a briefcase in one hand and a newspaper in the other. He sat opposite me and I was glad when he started to read his newspaper because I really didn't want to talk to anyone.

The journey, which was supposed to take an hour and a half, took longer because of a crash between two cars, one of which had landed on its roof. There were police cars and ambulances at the scene and the bus had to edge over to the side of the road along with all the other vehicles in the queue to allow a fire engine to pass.

The line of traffic moved slowly past, sometimes just a few inches at a time. The late-comer looked up from his paper to look at his watch and then he did it again a few minutes later. I guessed that he was going to be late for work. He must have decided that there wasn't a lot that he could do about it because he took a pen from his briefcase and started to do the crossword.

As we inched closer to the scene of the accident I could see the carnage. Several people had blankets around their shoulders and were standing together at the side of the road. I could see that someone else was lying on a stretcher in the back of the ambulance. There was a blanket over their head. And I'd thought that I had problems. There appeared to be death in the back of that ambulance; at least I had life inside me. My baby, a life, a living thing. I put my hands on my stomach and rocked with the motion of the slowly moving bus.

Once past the accident the bus picked up speed again and it wasn't long before we arrived at our destination. I got off and stretched while I looked around. I dug out the piece of paper that had the directions that Sharon had given me on and looked around for stand 21. It was easy enough to find and there was a bus due in fifteen minutes so I stood and waited.

When the time came, I asked the driver for a ticket to the end of Acton Road and asked him to tell me when we were there. I noticed that he gave me a sort of up and down look followed by a very slight nod of his head. He told me to sit down and listen for his shout. I took my ticket and sat near the front.

The bus pulled away and I settled into my seat. As I looked out of the window this new town that I had never seen before didn't look much different to the one that I had just left. There were people walking, others tending their gardens and mothers pushing prams.

'You need the next stop, love,' the driver called to me, looking at me through his rear-view mirror. 'This is Acton Road.'

As he slowed down I collected my things together and made my way to the exit. The bus stopped, the doors swished open and I climbed down the steps to the pavement. As the bus pulled away I looked at my directions again to try and work out which way to go and then I headed to my left.

\*\*\*

The building was set back from the road in its own grounds –
not massive grounds but bigger than your average garden.
There was nothing to suggest that it was anything other than
a normal, large house and I wondered if I'd got the right
place. I pushed the gate open, made sure that I closed it
behind me and walked up the path to the front door. I pushed
the bell and a few seconds later the door was opened by a
girl of about my age.

'I'm looking for Sharon,' I told her.

She looked me up and down in much the same way as the
bus driver had done. 'Sharon's not in,' she told me, 'but
Sophie is if she'll do.' She stepped back from the door.
'You'd better come in,' she said, so I did. As soon as I was
in she closed the door and yelled, 'Sophie! Someone to see
you.'

'Who is it?' the voice came from the second floor and
soon a face appeared at the top of the stairs. Its owner was
crouching down to see who it was that wanted her.

I tried to smile. 'Sharon told me to come,' I said
nervously.

'Oh.' A woman I took to be Sophie stood up straight and
ran down the stairs. 'You must be Susan.'

'Yes.'

'Right you are then, Susan,' she said, putting her hand on my back. 'You'd better come this way.' She turned to the girl who had let me in. 'Mandy, be a love and take Susan's bag upstairs.'

'Which room?'

Sophie let her head tilt to one side and smiled. 'Three guesses.'

Mandy picked up my bag and started the climb up the stairs.

I watched Mandy until she was halfway up the stairs and then followed Sophie into what looked like an office, although there were sofas in there too so I wasn't exactly sure what the room should be called. I would later learn that it was a room with many uses.

We didn't sit on the sofas that day. Sophie sat on one side of the desk and I sat on the other.

'So, Susan,' she said lightly. 'Tell me a bit about yourself.'

I didn't know what to say and shrugged my shoulders. 'There's not a lot to tell,' I said.

The look on Sophie's face told me that she had heard that before. 'Well, why don't we start with what brought you here?'

And that was all it took to start the waterfall of words that fell from my mouth. I told her about Tim and how we had already broken up before I'd found out that I was pregnant. I told her about Dad's disappointment and Mum's shame. I started crying when I told her that Mum had wanted to send me away until the baby was born and then give it way. Sophie offered me a box of tissues and, after I'd taken one, she gave me time to pull myself together – a process that took a few minutes.

When I was composed, Sophie said, 'I'm guessing that what your mother wants is not an option for you.' She was lolling to one side on her chair, as though she was quite comfortable. Her face was soft and friendly and she made me feel comfortable too. As we talked, she rummaged in one of the drawers of the desk and brought out a wedge of paper. She asked me a few questions then filled in a couple of forms which she asked me to sign.

'One last thing,' she said. 'Does anyone know you are here?'

'No.'

'Do you want anyone to know that you're here?'

'No.'

It seemed that was that.

***

When we were finished in the office, Sophie showed me to my room. It turned out I would be sharing a room with Mandy, the girl that had answered the door. There were two beds in what was to be my bedroom and I found Mandy sitting on one of them and my bag on the other.

I was blessed the day that Mandy came into my life. She became a good friend to me then and she is still a good friend to me now. That first evening, as we both sat on our respective beds, she explained to me how the hostel worked. Apparently the building had been donated to the charity by an old lady who had died without any children to pass the house on to. As the story went, the old lady had been pregnant and unmarried when she was young. Her family had disowned her and she'd been cast off with nowhere to go and no one to turn to. She had been forced to give birth to her baby in a dirty room somewhere, without any medical help, and had almost died as the baby was being born. The baby had died. Later on, her parents had relented a little – mainly for appearances' sake – and had taken her back, but she had never forgiven them for not being there for her when she needed them. When she died, the house and everything in it went to what was then a relatively new charity which had been set up to help young girls who found themselves in the same kind of trouble. Mandy told me she'd heard that a male cousin of the woman had tried to contest the will but the judge who had heard the case had told him where he could stick his objection.

'Bet it was a woman judge,' Mandy laughed, and I laughed too.

That first night we talked a lot. I told Mandy my story and she told me her own. They were similar in lots of ways but her mother hadn't suggested adoption; her father had suggested an abortion. We bonded straight away and I was glad that she was there with me. I was in a houseful of girls in the same predicament as I was and I felt at home.

Later on when Mandy was gently snoring a few feet away from me I lay in my bed and thought about the story of the old woman who had made this haven possible. I felt like we had something in common. We had both been let down by those who should have had our best interests at heart but, as bad as my case had been, hers had been so much worse. At least Mum had been going to send me somewhere safe. The old woman had just been turned out on the street, ostracised by her whole family – even the extended one – and, if that hadn't been bad enough, her baby had died. I couldn't imagine what that must have felt like and I didn't want to find out. Because of her I was here in a safe place and I thanked her from the bottom of my heart. Thank God I had found this place.

There were six bedrooms in the main building and four in an extension. Each bedroom could take two girls. We all chipped in with the cooking and cleaning and either Sophie or Sharon was there at all times. There was a third person who covered when one of them was on holiday or had a day off but Mandy wasn't sure what she was called. 'Daphne I think, or is it Daisy?'

I met most of the other girls around the dining table on my first evening in the house. Just after six a shout of, 'Tea's ready!' had gone up and I had followed Mandy into the dining room. We'd not had a dining room at home and I'd never sat at a dining table before, not in a house anyway.

Some of the girls had eyed me suspiciously as Mandy introduced me. Some of them were like me – just ordinary looking – others had bumps of various sizes and one girl, Gemma, looked like she was about to explode at any minute. My God, how could a body get that big? I couldn't imagine my stomach stretching so much and I wanted to ask her if it hurt but I didn't want to appear foolish.

So there we were, just a bunch of normal girls living in a big house together. Normal girls that just happened to be pregnant.

I fell into the way of life at the house – Sophie didn't like it being called a hostel – very quickly and within a few days I started to feel happy and positive about the future. Social Services worked with the charity that owned the house and someone from there came round at least once a week to check on us. We also had regular courses and talks about how to deal with what life was going to throw at us and it wasn't long before I started to believe that I could actually follow this path that I had chosen.

I realised that I could have this baby and I didn't care what it cost me personally.

I'd be lying if I said that I didn't think about the other path I could have chosen, the one that my mother had wanted, but I knew I had made the right decision. Every day I felt it more and more and I tried not to dwell on how things might have been.

I'm not going to bore you with details of everyday life at the house because that was just it, everyday life – mundane, some might even say dull. That was, apart from the times that one of us went into labour.

Gemma, the one who looked like she was going to pop, was – not surprisingly – the first of us to go into labour while I was there. It happened about a month after I got to the house. She'd been complaining about the odd twinge in her stomach all morning and just after lunch when Mandy and I were in the kitchen clearing up we heard her scream. The noise had come from the living room and by the time we got there Sharon was already on the floor beside the sofa that Gemma was sitting on. She was talking to someone on the phone, presumably the hospital.

'Okay, Gemma,' she said calmly, after she had put the phone back on its cradle. 'It looks like your baby is coming and an ambulance is on its way to take you to the hospital.' Sharon turned and looked at us. 'Can one of you go and get Gemma's hospital bag please. It's the red one by her bed.' She turned her attention back to Gemma and both Mandy and I ran up the stairs to Gemma's room.

Mandy was taking it in her stride, as she seemed to with most things, but this was my first experience of what happened to 'us girls' and I was really excited. By the time we got back downstairs the ambulance was pulling up outside and I opened the door before the engine had even stopped and showed the paramedics where to go.

While Mandy and I stood in the hallway and waited for them to do whatever it was that they were doing, I noticed that Mandy still had the red bag in her hand. It hadn't seemed right to go into the room once the paramedics had gone in. She handed the bag to Sharon as she came out of the room just ahead of the wheelchair that Gemma was sitting in.

'Okay, girls,' Sharon said. 'I've phoned Sophie to tell her what's happening and she'll be here in a few minutes, well half an hour or so. There's just the two of you in so do you think that you can look after yourselves until then?'

'Been doing it all my life, Shaz,' Mandy said in that bravado-ish way that she never really managed to pull off.

There was no bravado about Gemma though. She just looked terrified.

'Good luck, Gemma,' I said, forcing myself to smile. I didn't know what else to say or do.

Gemma didn't smile back; she screamed, 'Oh God it hurts.'

'Going to hurt a lot more before she's finished,' Mandy said softly out of the side of her mouth without moving her lips. Then she shouted, 'Yeah, good luck, Gemma. You'll be fine.'

We watched as Gemma was loaded into the back of the ambulance and Sharon climbed in after her. We stayed watching as it drove away and only closed the door once the ambulance had turned out of the short driveway.

By the time that Sophie arrived, about twenty minutes later, the dishes were all washed and put away, the kitchen benches were all wiped down and we were sitting on the sofa that Gemma had recently vacated.

'Hello, girls,' Sophie said in the bright and breezy way that she always used. 'Just us, is it?'

'Yeah,' Mandy said. 'Paula's at an antenatal class, Donna's at the dentist and the rest are out shopping, I think, apart from Caroline. She's gone to her reconciliation meeting.'

'Okay, I'll just put my things away,' and she left the room as quickly as she had entered it.

I had no idea what a reconciliation meeting was but I was willing to bet that Mandy would know. I had come to rely on her for all kinds of things and knowledge was one of them.

'What's a reconciliation meeting?' I asked.

'What?' she was flicking through a magazine.

'A reconciliation meeting. You said that Caroline was at her reconciliation meeting. What's one of them?'

'She's meeting her mother.'

'Her mother? I thought they didn't tell our parents.' Just the thought of it filled me with horror and I thought that I was going to be sick.

'They don't,' Mandy said. 'Not unless you decide you want them to.' She put her magazine on the table beside her and lay back on the soft cushions at the back of the sofa. 'I guess Caroline decided she wanted to see her mum after all. I thought she might.'

I lay back on my cushions too and thought about what Mandy had said. 'Do you think you'd want one?' I asked.

'What?'

'A reconciliation meeting.'

'With my mother?' She laughed out loud. 'Not likely. Not while my dad's still on the scene anyway. It was my mum who told me to get away from him. She told me to go and not tell her where because he would try to beat it out of her and if she didn't know, she couldn't tell him.' She turned to look at me. 'What about you?'

I was horrified by the thought of what Mandy had run away from. It got worse every time she mentioned her home life. 'What?' I said when I realised that she had asked me a question.

'Your mum. Will you want them to get in touch with her for you?'

'No,' I said without hesitation. 'Mum was so ashamed of me when I told her I was pregnant,' I said sadly. I think I was looking into space as I spoke; I certainly wasn't looking at Mandy. 'She wanted to hide me away, to send me to a cousin in Scarborough so that I could have the baby without the neighbours knowing. And then while I was gone she was going to arrange for it to be adopted.' I can still feel the tear that ran down my cheek, the one that I wiped it away quickly and hoped Mandy hadn't seen. 'Why would I want to see her again?'

'I know someone who had her baby adopted.' Mandy's tone was very matter of fact. 'Her mother talked her into it. You know the routine, said that a baby at her age would ruin her life blah, blah, blah. She said that she regretted it as soon as it was done and she cried every day for a month. She was on anti-depressants last time I saw her.'

'Not all it's cracked up to be, then?'

'Apparently not, though I guess it works for some people.' Mandy looked as though she was searching for the right words, which turned out to be, 'Was she really going to send you away?'

'Yes.'

'Bit old-fashioned isn't it? I thought they only did that years ago.'

'Mum is old-fashioned I suppose,' I said. 'Her idea of being of being a good wife and mother was to have a house that sparkled, clean clothes on the kids and her husband's tea on the table when he walked through the door. Everything had to look perfect to the outside world so, like I said, she was ashamed of me. She couldn't bear the thought of having a daughter who was an unmarried mother. What would the neighbours think? You've always got to consider what the neighbours will think.'

'How do you think she's explained this to them?'

'Explained what?'

'You running away.'

I hadn't really given it a lot of thought, though I was sure she'd have come up with something. 'No idea,' I said and, if I'm honest, I didn't really care. That was her problem.

Caroline came back about four o'clock and her mother waited in the office while she packed her bag. Sophie asked me to take Caroline's mum a cup of tea and when I did I found her sitting right where I'd been sitting earlier. That sofa had seen a lot that afternoon. I asked her if she wanted a biscuit but she said no, so I told her to give me a shout if she needed anything. I couldn't get out of the room quickly enough: she wasn't my mother but she might as well have been.

Caroline and her mother left about fifteen minutes after they'd arrived and as they walked away they both looked happy.

It was about nine o'clock when Sharon got back from the hospital. She told us that Gemma had had her baby boy just after six o'clock and was going to call him Peter. We never saw Gemma again, not in the house anyway. A few years later Mandy said she'd seen her and her little boy in a supermarket and that Gemma was pregnant again. She'd said that Peter had blond hair and a snotty nose.

After she left hospital with her baby, Gemma would have gone to a flat, some form of accommodation anyway, for her and her baby. That was how it worked. You were looked after in the house until your baby was born and after that you were out in the community fending for yourself. Well maybe it wasn't quite as bad as that: you were offered a lot of support and the really young girls went to a mother and baby unit, but after your baby was born you had to leave the house. The thought of leaving the house scared me but, as Mandy said, that was the way it had to be.

Mandy left the house for good one morning at the end of August. Her daughter was born that evening and Sophie took me to visit them both in hospital the next day. Mandy was sitting up in bed, propped up by pillows, and she smiled at us as we came in. My eyes were drawn to the plastic cot beside her bed where a tiny baby was fast asleep with her little fists up beside her ears. She was gently blowing bubbles out of pursed lips and she looked perfect.

'She's gorgeous,' I said.

113

'Takes after her mum,' Mandy laughed, and I laughed with her.

'I'm going to have a word with the Sister,' Sophie said, 'I'll not be long.'

I perched myself on the edge of the bed next to Mandy. 'What was it like?' I asked.

'Like trying to shit a cannon ball,' Mandy laughed.

'Oh.'

'Yes, "Oh!"' She grabbed my hand. 'It hurt like hell, Susan,' she said, 'but bloody hell it was worth it.' And when she looked at her baby, who was now awake and looking back at her, I knew that what she said was true. You could almost see the bond that had formed between the pair of them.

'What are you going to call her?' I asked.

'Jade,' she said. 'First of all because it's my favourite colour but also because it's precious,' Mandy stroked her daughter's arm, 'and so is she.'

I had never heard Mandy say anything so deep before – or since for that matter. It was odd going back to the house without her. In lots of respects things were just the same but without Mandy it felt different.

A couple of weeks after Jade was born I received a letter from Mandy giving me her new address. She said that she and Jade were settling in and getting along 'quite nicely'. She said she was enjoying her new role as a mother and I was happy for her.

My own time to leave came one rainy night in the middle of October. I'd been in bed for about ten minutes and had spent that time tossing and turning, first lying on one side and then the other. I'd tried puffing up the pillows and snuggling under the covers but I just felt so restless. And then suddenly there was a pain and I knew immediately that it was a contraction.

My stomach felt as though it was trapped in a vice that was being tightened and I frantically tried to remember what we had been taught in our antenatal lessons. I breathed slowly and deeply and waited for the pain to pass. They'd mentioned something with a long name that basically meant false labour – like they weren't real contractions, just pretend ones – so I decided to lie quietly for a while to see what would happen. What happened was that I had another contraction and then another a few minutes later.

I was so excited; scared obviously and more than a little anxious but most of all I was excited. It was happening, my baby was coming. What, or rather who, I had given up my family for was about to arrive and I couldn't wait to meet them.

I tried to sit up and it took a lot of effort but I made it. I sat on the side of the bed and tried to catch my breath.

'You okay?' Jenny, the girl who had taken Mandy's spot asked.

'I think the baby's coming,' I said.

'What should I do?' Jenny asked. She was younger than me and I could tell that she was terrified.

'Can you go and get Sharon, please,' I said.

She grabbed her dressing gown and was out of the door in seconds. I sat on the edge of the bed in the darkness and wondered what I should do next. For the first time since I'd arrived there I felt alone. Luckily for me, within a couple of minutes Sharon was sitting on the bed beside me, taking control of the situation. She had seen this many times before and she knew exactly what to do. She spoke to me gently and calmly, asking me about the contractions, how far apart were they and how long did they last? I told her as best I could.

'I think this is it,' Sharon said, squeezing my hand.

Oh my God, my heart was beating so fast. My mind went back to the day that Gemma had gone into labour and how Mandy had said that it would get much worse for her before it was over. And what was it that Mandy had said about her own delivery? That it was like passing – well, shitting – a cannon ball. I tried not to dwell on how much those first contractions had hurt.

I remembered what I'd overheard Mum saying to one of the neighbours a couple of years earlier. The daughter of someone in the street had had a baby and apparently it had been 'the worst labour ever', or at least that had been the new mum's opinion.

'Fuss about nothing,' Mum had said. 'Women have been having babies for thousands of years without all the fuss they make these days. It's natural and you just have to get on with it. You just have to get through the pain.'

I didn't know why it should bother me but I hoped that I would be able to bear the pain the way that Mum would expect me to.

I think that she would have been proud of me. I'm not going to try and tell you that it was easy because it wasn't. It hurt! But, for the most part, I found the pain bearable, especially with the gas and air mask to suck on – and God knows I sucked, especially towards the end.

'You'll hyperventilate,' one of the midwives said. Maybe I would, but I didn't care. Each lungful of the gas made me feel like I was rising towards the ceiling and then I would float gently back to the bed.

'Good stuff, isn't it,' Sharon said, as I moved the mask away from my mouth. And I had to agree with her. Then she pushed a stray hair away from my eyes as she asked, 'Do you want me to contact your family?'

What? I hadn't seen that one coming but now that it had … did I? I lay back into my pillow and waited for the next contraction to pass. 'Fuss about nothing.' Mum's words floated into my head.

'No,' I said definitely and Sharon left it at that. Mum was ashamed of me and my guess was that she had seen my disappearance as a lucky escape. She didn't have to hide me, hide my shame. It was me and my baby against the world and there was no place in that world for anyone who was ashamed of us. I knew that I was a disappointment to her and I accepted that. Sharon never mentioned it again.

My labour lasted a total of twelve and a half hours and just when I was starting to think that it was never going to end the midwife who was looking after me encouraged me to give 'one last push' and my beautiful baby was born. I heard her crying and I cried too when she was put into my arms for the first time.

She weighed eight pounds fifteen and a half ounces and she was perfect in every way. I held her in my arms and looked at her with wonder. I had done it! I had no idea that anything could ever be so beautiful and I felt like my heart was going to burst. This tiny little creature, my daughter, took my breath away.

'Do you have a name for her?' the midwife asked.

Did I? I can honestly say that I hadn't given it any thought. What was I going to call her? My mind went back to the night that I'd left home and to the candle that I'd lit in the church. 'Mary,' I said, 'her name is Mary.'

# JEAN

The Wednesday after Susan had told her us that she was pregnant Mick came home from work and said, 'Let's go for a drink tonight.' It took me by surprise a bit because we never went out together during the week. He sometimes went out on his own but I couldn't remember that last time he'd suggested we both go.

'You okay?' I asked, as I put his tea in front of him.

'Yeah,' he said, 'I just think we could both do with it.'

He wasn't wrong and I wasn't about to look a gift horse in the mouth.

I hadn't been sure about leaving Susan on her own, but she'd seemed a lot more settled that day, like she had come round to the idea of going to Scarborough. When we left she was watching television.

'Hello, Jean,' Gerry the barman, said when we walked in. 'We don't see you in here much on a week night. Special occasion is it?'

'Something like that,' I said.

'We are doing the right thing aren't we?' Mick said after we'd been sitting for a bit.

'Yeah,' I said. 'Course we are.' And we were, I was sure of it. What else could we do? Let her have the baby at home, you're probably thinking; if only it was that simple. I didn't want her to end up like me, trapped just because of a simple mistake. I know that Mick and me had been happy enough in our own way but, if I had been given my chance again, I'm not sure he would have been the one I'd choose to spend the rest of my life with. And no matter what people said about times being different, they weren't really; you still brought shame on yourself and your family when you found yourself pregnant without a ring on your finger. People talked about you, pointed fingers at you, and they weren't going to do that to my daughter. I realised that she didn't want to give her baby up but one day, when she was married to a nice bloke, living in a nice house, she'd thank me. There'd be other children and she'd be grateful that she hadn't thrown everything away. I'd had no choice; I'd had nowhere to go. I'd had to marry Mick and lie in the bed that I had made, but it could be different for Susan and I was going to make sure that it was.

We stayed in the pub for a couple of hours during which time Mick had had four pints and I'd had more than enough brandy and lemonade. I was glad that Mick had suggested going to the pub because for the first time in days, I felt relaxed. We stopped off at the chip shop on the way home and shared a bag of chips. We bought a bag for Susan. She deserved a treat. For the first time in years Mick and I were doing something together and I was almost happy. That soon changed when we got home.

The door was locked, which was a bit odd, and all the lights were off too so, at first, it just looked like Susan had gone to bed early. In the dark I stood on something, something hard, and after I'd put the light on I looked down to see what it was. When I saw the key – her key – on the floor, I knew something was wrong.

Mick said something like, 'Susan's dropped her key' and he picked up the heart-shaped key-ring that I had stood on. But I knew she hadn't dropped it and if it had fallen from the window sill where it usually sat it would have been on the floor beneath it, not behind the door directly underneath the letter box.

'She must be in bed,' Mick said and I told him that I'd go and check.

I felt sick when I saw that her bed was empty and before I knew it I was on the floor looking under the bed for the bag she'd had for the school trip to Wales. I almost didn't dare to look in her wardrobe. I opened the door slowly and found that some of her clothes were gone – not many, but enough. I washed, ironed and put her clothes away so I knew what should be in there. I knew I wasn't imagining it.

'Mick,' I shouted at the top of my lungs and he came running up the stairs like he was going to find that his baby had topped herself and was lying dead on the bed. 'She's gone,' I said and could see the relief wash over his face. 'She's gone,' I said and I dropped down onto her bed.

'What do you mean?' he asked.

All I could do was laugh. 'What do you think I mean? She's gone. She's packed some clothes and she's gone.'

I opened the drawer of the bedside cabinet and rummaged through it. She kept her bank book in there and I went through everything three times before I had to accept that it wasn't there. I tried to remember how much had been in there the last time I'd looked but I wasn't sure of the exact amount. I didn't think it had been a lot. She'd got some money for Christmas but I knew that she'd spent some of that on records so she couldn't have much left. But where had she gone? And why? We had a plan; we were going to sort things out. She had no reason to run away. Where the hell could she have gone?

Julie's. She had to have gone to Julie's.

Mick was standing in the doorway just looking around the room as though he was hoping to see her hiding in a

123

corner and I had to virtually push him out of the way to get out of the room. I ran downstairs and picked up the phone. When Julie answered, she sounded sleepy. I looked at the clock and realised that I had probably woken her up.

'Is Susan there?' I asked

'No. Why would she be?' I could hear her yawning.

'Because she's not here,' I told her.

'What?' That had woken her up.

'Me and your dad went out for a drink,' I told her, 'and when we came back we found her key on the floor. Your dad thought she must have locked the door and gone to bed but when I checked, her bed was still made, her bag is gone and so are some of her clothes.'

'Where could she have gone?'

'You tell me,' I snapped

'How should I know?' Julie snapped back.

'I thought she might have gone to you or at least told you where she was going. I mean you were as thick as thieves the other afternoon.'

'We're sisters and she was in trouble,' Julie said defiantly.

*Yeah, well, she is now,* I thought, or at least she would be when we found her.

124

Neither of us said anything else for a bit and all I could hear was breathing on the other end of the line. I heard what sounded like a big sigh from Julie's end of the phone and I could imagine her blowing the air out her cheeks: she'd done it all her life.

'You don't think she'll have gone to Helen's, do you?' I asked and I was horrified just thinking she might have.

Julie asked why on earth Susan would have gone to Helen, but I needed to be sure so I rang Helen's anyway. By this time Mick had come downstairs and he stood in the doorway watching me. The phone rang about half a dozen times before it was picked up.

'No,' Helen said in answer to my question. 'Why would Susan be here?'

Bugger. What was I going to tell her? I hadn't thought it through. I'd been so fixed on finding out where Susan was that I hadn't thought about what I would say if Helen said she wasn't.

'Mum,' Helen said slowly, 'why are you ringing me at this time of night to ask if Susan's here?'

I could hear Robert's voice in the background, not what he was saying, just his voice. His mother would have a field day with this when word got out. A right snob she was.

'Mum?' Helen said again.

There was nothing for it, I took a deep breath and said, 'We had a bit of a row earlier.'

'What about?' It was a natural enough question but I wasn't going to answer it just then.

'Nothing, really,' I lied, 'but Susan must have got a nark on about it because she's packed a bag and disappeared while we were out.'

'Out? It's not like you to go out on a Wednesday.'

'Yes, well, we did tonight.'

'She's probably shacked up with a mate somewhere.' Helen yawned as she spoke, then she gave a little cough before she said. 'Can't believe it of Susan, though. I didn't know she had it in her.'

Neither did I.

'Anyway, Mum, I'm going to have to go,' Helen said, 'the baby's crying.'

'Sorry I woke you. Goodnight.'

'They don't know where she is,' I said.

And before I had chance to say anything else Mick asked, 'You did tell her didn't you?'

'Tell her what?'

'Don't give me that, Jean, because I know you too well. You know fine well what I'm talking about.' He stared at me but I couldn't look at him. 'You didn't tell her, did you?'

I could hear the anger in his voice. Every word was a bit louder than the one before it.

'You didn't tell her that she wouldn't have to give her baby up did you.'

My mouth was opening, I know it was, but nothing came out.

'For fuck's sake, Jean,' he grabbed his coat from where he had thrown it and pushed his arms into it. 'We said that she wouldn't have to give it up, not if she didn't want to.' Mick didn't swear, not in front of me anyway. I had only ever heard him use that word once before and that was the day that I'd told him I was expecting Helen. There was something in his eyes as he looked at me and I can only describe it as dark. 'I let you talk me into sending her away but we could have come up with a way of letting her keep it.'

'How?' I finally bit back. 'How could we? Do you really want her being the talk of the place? Do you really think that her life would be anything but ruined if she kept it?'

'Is that what your life was?' his hand was on the door handle.

'Times were different then,' I said. 'You got pregnant, you either went to that old witch at the bottom of Hagg Lane or you got married, simple as that.' I stood up to go to him but the look on his face and that rising temper of his stopped me. 'I was happy to marry you, Mick, but do you really want her hooked up to that Preston lad for the rest of her life? Mick,' I pleaded, 'I was only thinking of what was best for her.'

'You were thinking of what the neighbours would think Jean Bradley,' he was spitting the words at me. 'That's always been the thing with you, getting one up on the neighbours, being better than them. I just never thought that you'd put that before your own daughter.' He shook his head, opened the door and walked through it.

'I'll stay here in case she comes back,' I said but the door had closed before I'd even finished speaking.

His words had hit me hard and I could feel tears starting to rise up. I wasn't sure then, and I'm still not sure now, which of his words hurt me the most. Was it what he'd said about me putting what the neighbours might think before the needs of my own daughter or was it the fact that he called me Jean Bradley? Why had he done that? At that point we'd been married the best part of thirty years. He was hurting and he knew exactly what to say to make me hurt too.

He was wrong about one thing though. Whether he liked it or not my name was Thompson, Jean Thompson. As for putting what the neighbours thought before my daughter, maybe I had but in my book appearances were everything.

And I hadn't put them first, I just hadn't wanted them to see our dirty laundry.

What was wrong with him? He had a good name on this estate, people always said what a good bloke he was or what a nice house and family he had and most of that was down to me. What the neighbours thought or said was important to everyone and anyone who denied that was living in cloud cuckoo land.

There was nothing else to do but put the kettle on and drink endless cups of tea while I sat at the kitchen table and waited. I racked my brains to try and come up with some idea of where she might be. Helen had said that she'd be at a friend's but I didn't think that was very likely; Susan didn't have many friends. I mean, there had been that lass that she'd been to a couple of parties with a while back but I didn't even know what she was called. It might have been Margaret, or was it Maureen? It could have been Martha for all I knew. It was just someone she knew from school and anyway I was sure I'd heard Susan say that they'd moved to Scotland or somewhere. Something about her dad getting a job on the oil rigs. I don't think I'd ever heard her mention anyone else. I kicked myself for not paying more attention when she'd been telling me stuff.

Where had she gone the silly girl? And why had she done it? Well, I suppose I knew the answer to that one. Mick was right; it was the adoption thing. She'd had the notion in her head that she would be able to have her baby and bring it up herself and life would be just wonderful. She had no idea.

Yes, she could have the baby. Yes, she could bring it up herself but she would forever be known as 'that lass that fell wrong' and I didn't want that for her. If she was honest she wouldn't want it for herself. I was giving her a way out. I was giving her a chance at having the life that she really wanted for herself. Why could she not see that?

'Why, Susan?' I shouted.

An unwanted pregnancy I could cover up, I'd seen plenty of others do it, but this? I had no idea what to do with this.

I watched the door and the clock in equal measures; watched the minutes tick by and waited for the door to open. One time, my eyes were drawn to the bag of chips that we'd bought for Susan. They were sitting on the bench where I had left them before I ran up the stairs. I couldn't even be bothered to get up and throw them in the bin, so I went back to watching the clock and the door.

I felt sick – actually, physically sick – and I prayed to God that Mick would find her.

***

When he came through the door just after midnight, I knew that my prayers hadn't been answered. He walked in alone and closed the door.

'Any sign of her?' I asked, more in hope than expectation.

'No,' he said. His head was down and his chin almost touched his chest. I thought I heard him make a sound. I think it was a sob. I felt so sorry for him.

When he lifted his head up he had that darkness in his eyes again. 'You got your wish,' he said. 'She's gone away and who knows if she's ever coming back? You can tell the neighbours what you want, but you'd better tell Sally that I won't be there on Sunday.'

I didn't know what to say, so I asked, 'Do you want a cup of tea?'

'Yeah, why not? That'll make everything all right.' He fell onto one of the kitchen chairs and rested his elbows on the table so that he could put his head in his hands.

I filled the kettle, washed the teapot out and got two fresh mugs out of the cupboard. I had just filled the teapot with the boiling water and was about to pick it up when it was as if the teapot had suddenly become too heavy for me to pick up because although I grabbed the handle I couldn't lift it. I suddenly felt faint and had to put both hands on the bench to support myself. A thought had just occurred to me.

'She won't have gone to *him*, will she?'

When I turned around, Mick still had his head in his hands. 'I don't know where she's gone,' he said.

I managed to pour the tea and put one of the mugs in front of Mick. I put the other one on the opposite side of the table and sat down. We didn't say a lot and we didn't drink much tea either. Eventually I asked Mick where he had looked and he just said, 'Around.' I wanted to ask him where exactly but his answers were vague. I put that down to his head being all over the place.

Just before two I said, 'Come on, Mick. Let's go to bed. You look knackered.' And I got up from my chair and went to lock the door.

'Leave it,' he said and I put the key that had been in my hand back down. 'Susan hasn't got her key,' he said as he pushed his chair back and it made a scraping sound along the floor.

We went to bed but neither of us slept. As I lay awake and watched a different clock tick off the minutes till morning all I could think about was Susan and where she might be. Where was she sleeping? Was she sleeping at all? She'd certainly made sure that I wasn't.

I'd always thought that I knew my daughters and that nothing they could do would surprise me because I was always one step ahead of them but, good God, Susan surprised me that night. I hadn't seen this coming. She had never done anything like it before in her life. She had never defied me before. That girl could pick her bloody moments.

I wished that I hadn't gone out that night. I'd never have thought of doing it if Mick hadn't suggested it. He mustn't have seen it coming either.

I must have dozed off at some point because when the alarm went off it startled me and I didn't feel any better for the little sleep I'd had. I heard the sound of the toilet flush being pulled and for a second I thought that I'd woken up from a bad dream and that Susan had been at home all the time. But when I turned over and saw Mick walking back into the bedroom, I could tell from the look on his face that we were still living the nightmare.

\*\*\*

Mick had just gone to work when the phone rang and my heart was in my mouth as I ran to the hallway to pick it up. Was it Susan? Was it the hospital or maybe even the police saying that she had done something stupid? All of this was going through my head in the five seconds that it took me to get to the phone. I looked at it for two more rings because I was scared to pick it up, scared of who it was and what they might say. In my head, I can still see my hand shaking as I picked the receiver up.

It was Julie wanting to know if Susan had come home.

'No,' I said, 'she hasn't. I don't know what she thinks she's playing at.'

We spent a couple of minutes sparring which was all me and Julie ever seemed to do in those days. She wanted to know what we had said to Susan, what support we had offered her.

'You did let her know that everything was going to be all right, didn't you?' Julie said. 'I mean, I know she'd have to give up her exams but it wasn't going to be the end of the world.'

Julie would be thinking like that though. I knew that she and Chris were trying for a baby so being pregnant wouldn't be the end of the world for her. But Susan wasn't her. I didn't think that was the time to tell Julie about the plan to send Susan to Sally's until she'd had the baby, and I certainly wasn't going to say anything about adoption.

'Hopefully she'll be home soon,' was the last thing that Julie said, but I was starting to have my doubts.

On any other Thursday morning I would have been cleaning the windows but that day I sat at the table and prayed. Though I'd been raised Catholic, and I'd had all the girls baptised, I'd not been much of a one for church in recent years but I didn't know what else to do. I'm not exactly sure what it was that I was praying for, maybe it was that Susan would come back so that at least we could control the situation, but more likely it was to go back to a time when there was no situation to control. And that was when the thought came to me. Maybe Susan had gone to make the situation disappear. I don't really hold with abortion, and I'd always said that, so maybe Susan had gone somewhere she could get an abortion without me knowing. Was she trying to make the situation disappear? To my shame now, I hoped she was and I think in my heart that, for a second at least, that was what I was praying for: that there'd be no hiding and explaining and she could come back and carry on as normal. She could put the whole thing behind her and pretend it had never happened.

It didn't take me more than a few seconds to work out that she couldn't have done that. I mean, she didn't want to give it away so there was no way she'd let anyone kill it and I hated myself for even thinking that she might do something like that. She just wouldn't. I prayed some more, repeating the words that I'd been taught as a child and thought I'd forgotten.

135

Just before eleven the phone rang again and once more my legs shook as I walked the few yards to the hallway. I hoped that it would be Susan but, judging by the time, I thought it would most probably be Mick, on his break, checking to see if she had come home. I got the shock of my life when a woman said, 'Hello, is that Mrs Thompson?'

Oh my God! Was it the hospital or the police? It had to be one of them.

'Yes?' I managed to whisper.

'Oh, hello Mrs Thompson. I'm sorry to bother you, but this is Miss Ford, Susan's form teacher. I just wondered if Susan would be in school this afternoon.'

I think I said 'Sorry' or 'Excuse me' or something like that because the next thing Miss Ford was saying was, 'It's just that, as you know Mrs Thompson, Susan is in the middle of her exams. Now I know that they're called mock exams but that doesn't mean that they're not important…'

I remembered Miss Ford – not much more than a kid herself. When we'd met her at the last parents' evening both me and Mick had agreed that she didn't look old enough to be a teacher.

'…So can you tell me if Susan will be in?'

She'd caught me on the hop. 'No Miss Ford. She won't. Susan's not feeling very well today.'

136

She started to say something else but I cut her off. 'I'm really sorry Miss Ford,' I said, 'but I'm going to have to go.'

'But will Susan be in tomorrow?'

'I'm not sure. Goodbye,' and I put the phone down. I don't know what she must have thought of me but she had caught me unprepared. I kicked myself for being so stupid. Why had I not remembered Susan's exams and thought to ring the school to say that she wouldn't be in?

They had a policy now of checking on kids that didn't turn up at school. There'd been a letter come home about it. It was something about cutting down on the number of truancy days. Now, thanks to me forgetting to ring them, they'd had to ring me and that would be a mark against Susan's name.

'Not feeling very well.' Was that the best I could come up with? I know you're probably wondering why it mattered about Susan getting a mark against her name, because she wasn't going back to school anyway, and maybe it wouldn't matter to some, but it did to me. My kids were never in detention and they didn't get marks against their names at school. Some kids stayed home from school at the fist sign of a sniff, but not mine. My girls always had good attendance records. I knew that I would have to deal with the school again but right at that moment I couldn't think about that.

For the first time in all our married life, Mick came home to his tea not being on the table that night. It wasn't my fault really because he'd knocked off work an hour early. I commented on it when he came in.

'You're early,' I said, 'your tea's not on yet.'

'It's all right,' he said walking straight through the kitchen to the stairs. 'I'm not hungry.'

That told me everything that I needed to know about how he was feeling because Mick was always hungry. Even after he'd just eaten a big meal he'd be hungry again within the hour. I'd never known him not be hungry but, more than that, I'd never known him finish work early.

He'd not been back long when the lasses turned up mob-handed with their men.

'Is she back?' Julie asked before she was even through the door. She only had to look at our faces to see the answer. Helen, hot on her heels, asked the same question and reached the same conclusion.

Julie gave a nod of her head which sent Chris and Robert off to the living room while she and Helen sat at the table with us.

'What's going on?' Helen said. 'What aren't you telling us?'

Julie couldn't keep her mouth shut. 'Susan's pregnant.'

'What? Whose is it?' Helen looked at me first, then her dad and finally Julie who wasted no time in telling her who the father was.

'Oh.' The noise sort of popped out of Helen's mouth. My eyes were cast down looking at the table but I could feel Helen looking at me. It was like her eyes were burning holes into the top of my head. After a few seconds I looked up at her.

'But why would she run away?' Helen asked. 'Where is she?'

'We don't know,' I said. 'Your dad went out looking for her as soon as we found out she was missing but he couldn't find her.'

'Where did you look, Dad?' she asked and I was glad that she'd turned her attention somewhere else. I saw a different side to Helen that night. She was demanding answers and that was something she had never done before. She had never been that sort of girl, not where her dad was concerned anyway.

139

He shrugged his shoulders. 'Just around really. I walked up the back for a bit and down towards the bus station, but there was no sign of her.'

We all knew why he had gone where he said he had.

'Was she there?' Julie asked. 'Has he seen her?'

Mick pushed himself away from the table and stood up. He walked to the sink and poured himself a glass of water. We all watched him take a large gulp and put the glass down. 'I saw Tim Preston with his hand inside Lisa Donnelly's blouse,' Mick said, and we could all hear the pain in his voice. He was probably imagining that low-life doing a similar thing to Susan and that wasn't a picture any of us wanted in our heads.

'Does he know?' Helen asked me, almost under her breath.

'No,' I said, shaking my head. I was talking to her but I was looking at Mick. I didn't like his colour and I hoped that he wasn't going to have a heart attack.

'He wasn't acting like he knew,' Mick said, as he leaned heavily against the sink and took a couple of deep breaths.

I walked over to Mick and tried to look into his eyes. 'You all right, love?' I asked. He didn't say whether he was or he wasn't but he straightened himself up, turned around and faced the girls who were looking just as worried about him as I was.

'She hasn't been to his,' I said. 'She was on about telling him, but I don't think she has because if she had we'd have had his mother round here by now.'

They all knew that I was right. I was glad when Mick sat down again. I still didn't like the way he looked and I was scared that he might fall down if he stayed on his feet. We sat around the table for a while and talked, though it felt more like an interrogation than a conversation. I didn't know where all this sisterly concern had come from because Helen had barely looked at Susan when she lived at home. Now she was banging on about being concerned for her baby sister. It would have been funny if it hadn't been so serious.

They stayed for about an hour and then the four of them disappeared to the pub. Robert's mum was babysitting so they were going to make the most of it. We didn't bother much after the girls had gone. The tea that I had been going to cook wasn't made so we had a sandwich and a cup of tea and went to bed early, though God knows why because it would be another sleepless night.

*** 

A couple of nights after Susan had gone, Julie turned up again just after I'd washed up. She walked into the kitchen and Chris followed her, closing the door behind him. He tried to force a smile in my direction and I tried to force one back. We both failed miserably. He was a good lad Chris. I hadn't been so sure about him when Julie first brought him home but he'd turned out all right.

I could see that Julie had something in her hand. 'Where's Dad?' she asked.

Before I had a chance to say that he was in the living room he appeared at the doorway. He must have heard the sound of voices and come to see who was there. He couldn't hide his disappointment when he realised that it wasn't the daughter that he wanted to see.

'Hello, love,' he said, but his heart wasn't really in it.

'This came today,' she said as she gave what she'd been holding to her dad.

I could see now that it was an envelope, one of the small white ones, not the type that official stuff comes in but the type that you can get in any newsagent. I saw the little colour he had drain from his face as he looked at it. His hands were shaking as he slowly took the letter out of the envelope and read it. Once he had, he handed it to me. I immediately recognised Susan's handwriting. I will never forget the words that were written on that piece of paper.

*Dear Julie*, it said, *I am so sorry that I left without saying goodbye. Thank you for everything but I can't let them take my baby away so if that means leaving without telling anyone where I'm going, that's what I've got to do. Don't worry about me, I'll be fine. I have a plan and I know what I'm doing. Please tell them not to look for me because I don't want to be found. Look after yourself Julie, and them too.* There were three *x*'s at the end.

When I'd read the letter twice more I looked up to see that Julie and Mick were both watching at me. Chris had disappeared and the three of us stood together in the kitchen just looking at each other.

***

About a week after Susan had gone Julie was waiting for me on the doorstep when I got home with the groceries. She was talking to Ida Watson from over the road. They stopped talking as I got closer.

'All right, Jean?' Ida said. 'I was just saying to your Julie that I haven't seen Susan for a bit. Is she okay? Not poorly is she?'

I hoped that the horror that I was feeling didn't show in my face.

'No,' I said, 'not poorly. She's just gone away for a bit.'

'On holiday?'

143

The words were out of my mouth before I knew it. 'Not a holiday, as such,' I said. 'Mick has an aunt in Scarborough and Susan's gone to stay with her for a bit. She hasn't been well, so Susan's gone to look after her.'

I could see Ida's mind ticking over as she thought about what I had just told her. 'But wasn't she doing her exams soon?'

'Yes,' I said, 'but you know how it is, Ida; she can always take them another time. Family comes first.'

'That's very good of her,' Ida said as she started to walk away. 'Tell her I said hello next time you talk to her. Nice talking to you, Julie.'

I was kidding myself if I thought that Ida had believed me. It'd take her no time at all to work out the truth because she'd used the same excuse herself. Her middle daughter had once gone to 'look after her grandma' for the best part of a year. If Ida knew, it wouldn't be long before the whole street knew. And it wasn't; it took just a couple of days.

I knew that they knew and they knew that I knew that they knew, if you know what I mean. Nobody mentioned it directly but we all knew what was gong on. It was like a game that we all played. It wasn't the first time that we had played it and I was sure that it wouldn't be the last.

144

Except it was a slightly different game we were playing this time, because Susan wasn't hiding away at a relative's house until her baby was born; we had no idea where she was.

***

I had an aunt who used to say that when you were going through a hard time you just had to breath through it until it passed so that's what I did. The trouble was that it didn't seem to be passing. Mc and Mick were barely talking; I knew he blamed me for what had happened and, to be honest, I could see why he would. None of this would be Susan's fault. Nothing was ever Susan's fault.

Helen was too wrapped up in her own life to pay too much attention to what was happening in ours. So much for her concern for her baby sister. She wanted to distance herself from our embarrassment I suppose. She had Robert's mother to consider. Robert's mother hadn't been that keen on us as a family to start with; she'd always thought Helen wasn't good enough for her precious son and this would be all the proof that she would need. What a mess.

Julie at least did show some concern. 'Have you called the police?' she asked one day when she had popped in on her way home from work. We hadn't. 'Do you not think that you should?'

145

'Your dad won't hear of it,' I said.

'What? Why? I'd have thought he'd want them out day and night looking for her.'

I'd thought the same myself but Mick had been adamant. 'What's the point?' he'd said. 'We know why she's run away and she's written us a note saying that she doesn't want to be found. They won't be able to force her to come home so I can't see them breaking their necks to find her.'

I told Julie what her dad had said.

'He's got a point I suppose,' Julie said, and I agreed with her. But I hadn't really understood Mick's reaction and I think she probably felt the same.

'She'll be all right you know, Mum,' Julie said, with more compassion than I'd ever heard in her voice before.

In my heart I agreed with her. Susan would be all right because, for a stupid girl, she was sensible. She was certainly the most sensible daughter I had.

***

I kept breathing and time kept passing. Days became weeks and then gradually turned into months.

We didn't hear from Susan or at least me and her dad didn't. Julie said she hadn't, but who knew? If Susan had asked Julie not to tell us she wouldn't. I hoped that the girls were in contact with each other. Like I think I told you, they had become close recently and Julie was taking Susan's disappearance very badly.

'Shouldn't we at least look for her,' she said one Sunday when she and Chris came round for their dinner.

We'd been eating in silence all the way through the roast beef and Yorkshire puddings and Julie brought the subject up while I was dishing up rhubarb crumble. I kept my head down and carried on putting food on plates.

'I mean,' Julie pressed the point when nobody answered her, 'Susan's been gone for months.'

I couldn't hide by the cooker all day so I slowly carried the four bowls of steaming crumble and custard to the table and put them down. Chris dealt with what was going on like he did most things involving the Susan situation; he let us get on with it. He picked his spoon up and started tucking in. Mick picked his up too but just stirred his food, while Julie held her spoon like a weapon.

'She said she doesn't want to be found,' Mick said, as he carried on stirring.

I could see a rage building behind Julie's eyes. She was frustrated and when she was frustrated she got angry. I knew that and so did Chris. I saw him give her a sideways glance but he must have decided she was okay because he carried on eating and his wife carried on staring at her father.

'She might have changed her mind.' Julie said.

'Then she can come home.' Mick finally started to eat his food.

'How?' Julie asked flinging her spoon onto the table in her temper.

'Same way she left.' Mick's voice was flat, emotionless.

'She won't,' Julie pushed the chair away from the table. 'She won't and you know it. And do you know why?' She had grabbed her coat from the back of the chair and started putting it on. 'She won't because she's ashamed.' She was fastening her coat up all wrong but she didn't care, she was in full flow. 'She's ashamed that you're ashamed of her. Because I'm willing to bet that's what you told her, wasn't it?'

She directed the question at me. I didn't deny it.

'Well she has,' I said.

'What? We're not living in the Dark Ages, Mam,' she said. '*She* hasn't brought shame on us, but *you* have. You've brought shame on us by forcing her to run away. Don't you get her? Susan is clever…'

'She wasn't very clever when she got pregnant.'

Julie stared at me defiantly. 'She's not the first … Is she?' She took a deep breath, gave Chris the nod and waited for him to get his own coat. 'As I was saying, Susan is clever and she is kind. She didn't want to be pregnant, but she was and she was willing to face up to her responsibilities. She wouldn't have wanted you to make it go away; she would have wanted you to help her.'

'Help her? What do you think we were trying to do?' My own temper was starting to rise now.

'You wanted her to give her baby away.' Chris had his coat on by that point and was by the door. Julie was beside him. 'She couldn't even give her dolls away, Mam, so how the hell did you expect her to give her baby up?'

And then they were gone.

'She's right, you know,' Mick had given up all pretence of eating the crumble and had pushed the bowl away. 'Susan would never have given her baby away.'

I looked down at my own, untouched food.

'You left her with no choice.'

I tried to open my mouth to defend myself but I didn't get the chance.

'You forced her away, Jean. You forced her to do what she did. You didn't tell her that she didn't have to give her baby away and she felt like she had no choice but to leave.'

His voice had been low and flat before but it grew louder and angrier. I wanted to tell him to keep his voice down

149

because the whole street would be able to hear him but I didn't get the chance before he was at me again.

'Why the hell did I ever let you talk me in to ringing Sally? Why didn't we just hold her and tell her that everything was going to be all right? Why didn't you tell her that she didn't have to give the baby up if she didn't want to?' Then, just as Julie had before him, he scraped his chair back from the table and stood up. Though Julie certainly had his temper, hers was just a baby version. I was about to be on the end of Mick's full fury.

'But do you know the question I ask the most Jean?' he was taking deep breaths and I couldn't bear to look at the rage on his face. 'Do you? Do you?'

I shook my head as I sat trembling in the chair.

'I ask myself why the hell I ever married you,' he yelled.

'Because you got me pregnant,' I yelled back. That stopped him in his tracks.

'So that you didn't have to give your baby way.'

'And is that what you want for Susan?' I tried to control my voice. 'Things were different then.'

'And they could have been different for her.' His voice was calmer too but it didn't scare me any less. He moved to the living room door and stood there with his back to me. 'I saw her you know,' he said.

'Saw her? What do you mean you saw her? When did you see her?'

'The night she ran away. I saw her the night she ran away.'

I got up from my chair, grabbed hold of his arm and forced him to look at me. 'What do you mean? Where did you see her? Why didn't you bring her back?'

'Bring her back?' There were tears rolling down Mick's cheeks, something I had never seen before. He looked down at me. 'Why would I bring her back here' he said slowly, 'to you?' As he shook his head the tears fell off the end of his chin. 'I didn't bring her back; I didn't even speak to her. I just gave her my blessing and walked away.'

Then he walked away from me too.

I sat for a long time in the kitchen thinking about what Mick had said. I knew he was telling the truth when he said that he'd seen Susan. It explained everything, why he was so vague about where he had been when he went to look for her, why he didn't want to go to the police. I'd known that there was something he wasn't telling me and now I knew what it was. He'd as much as said that Susan would be better off without me. He'd let his Susan disappear just so that she could get away from me. What did he think I was? A monster? I wasn't a monster. I loved Susan, in my own way.

I know some might find that hard to believe, but it's true. She was my baby as much as his.

But she was gone now. Like me and her dad, Susan was lying in the bed that she had made and I hoped that she was happy with it.

***

We found a way to live with each other. If he'd been honest about it – which he wasn't – Mick was just as bothered about keeping up appearances as I was. There had never been a divorce in either of our families and we weren't going to be the first, so we had to make the best of it. It wasn't easy at first – well, not later on either – but we found a way.

Julie was a bit harder to deal with but it wasn't long before she had something else to worry about. She was pregnant. At last, she was having a baby herself.

We were all happy for her, of course, but that night – the night she told us – I'm willing to bet that I wasn't the only one who was thinking about Susan, wondering where she was and how she was doing. How far along would she have been by then? Six months, seven maybe?

When I was out and about, the odd person would ask about Susan; you know, was she still in Scarborough, when was she coming home, that sort of thing.

'Oh she's fine, thank you,' I used to say. 'Loves it. In fact, she's talking about moving there.'

Well, if she wasn't coming back I had to tell them something.

I had ticked the weeks off in my head and I knew that Susan, wherever she was, would be coming close to her time. I wasn't sure exactly when she was due but when she'd been gone for eight months I knew that her time had passed. She would have her baby by now.

## SUSAN

I lay on my side in the hospital bed and watched Mary as she slept in the plastic cot beside me. Her tiny arms were high over her head and her feet moved in time to a silent rhythm. First one and then the other kicked out: kick, kick, kick and kick – one, two, three and four. My daughter was already dancing to her own tune.

My baby girl. I had a baby girl. I was a mother. I'd done it and I could hardly believe it. I may have been little more than a child myself – I was basically a child with a child – but she was mine and I knew that I would love her forever, protect her from anything and even give my life for hers if I had to. I knew the bed that I had made, as Mum would say, and I was happy to lie in it; it was fine by me because Mary and I would be in it together.

Later, as I held Mary in my arms and gently rocked her to sleep, I thought – not for the first time that day – about my own mother. Surely she must have felt this way when we were born? Oh, but maybe not, because I remembered that she hadn't wanted me, but she must have with the other two.

I looked around the four-bed ward that I was in and tried to gauge how the other mums felt about their new arrivals. I was in the corner by the window and could see them all clearly.

The woman next to me was probably in her thirties and told me that she had just had her fifth son. She'd spoken to me as soon as I'd been settled on to the ward and asked me how I was and what I'd had, that sort of thing. When I told her that I'd had a baby girl, she laughed and asked me what my secret was.

'Just had my fifth bloody lad,' she said nodding towards where he lay in his cot. 'Fifth for goodness' sake, that's nearly half a football team. Never mind, there's always next time.'

Next time!

'Just kidding love,' she laughed, 'he's my last.'

The woman opposite me looked about the same age and she'd had a baby boy too. She told us that it was her first baby and that she and her husband had been trying for one for years. She called him their 'blessing from God'.

The woman next to her was a bit younger than the other two I would have said, but certainly older than me. She'd had her baby girl a few days before I'd had Mary and the

155

woman in the bed next to me, the one with the five boys, told me that she'd never once seen her pick her daughter up.

Even when the baby cried she didn't picked it up and when it was hungry a nurse would come and feed it.

'Post-natal depression,' the woman next to me said. I wish that I could remember her name but I'm not very good with names. 'I've seen it before,' she said. 'I had it when our so and so was born, he was my third. I never saw him go hungry like that though. I still fed him and kept him clean. I just couldn't stand the bloody sight of him till he was six months old.'

I was a bit embarrassed because I couldn't see how the woman opposite could help but hear what was being said about her.

Later, when the others were sleeping I lay back on my pillow, looked out of the window and thought about what the woman next to me had said about not being able to stand the sight of her baby until he was six months old. How could such a thing happen? I felt as though I could spend the rest of my life just looking at Mary. I couldn't understand how any mother, including my own, could not feel the same way as I did and I pitied them. I pitied them because this was the best feeling in the world.

Visiting time started at two and I was pleased when I saw Sharon appear at the door with a teddy bear in her hand. When she was close enough she reached over and gave me a big hug.

'Well done love,' she said, before turning her attention to my baby. 'Who's this then? Have you decided?' she asked.

'Mary,' I said with pride.

Sharon could only stay about half an hour because she needed to get back to the house. I was sadder than I had ever imagined I would be when she said that, because I knew that I wouldn't be going back there. Where would I – we – be going? I asked Sharon.

'My guess would be to a flat in Palmer's Court,' she said, 'near Mandy. But don't get your hopes up too much,' she continued. 'It'll depend on whether there's an opening there or not. It'll be somewhere like that though. Someone will come and see you about it in the next couple of days.'

I remember her looking at her watch and then checking the time against the clock that was on the wall above the window. She apologised and said that she would have to go. She gave me a hug and stroked Mary's cheek before she left. I have never seen Sharon again since.

The following afternoon they had a visiting session that was just for fathers. One of the nurses said something about it being a chance for both parents to bond with their new baby. Obviously there was no father to visit my baby so I pretended to read a magazine but was really looking over the top of it to see how the fathers were getting on with their bonding session.

I heard the one on my right suggesting that they try again for a girl, but his wife was having none of it. Over her dead body was how she put it. The one opposite looked as pleased as Punch, so proud of his achievement that he spent the entire time kissing his wife and his baby in turn. The husband of the woman diagonally opposite me spent his time trying to coax his wife to even look at their baby.

I thought about Tim and wondered how different things might have been. I wondered if I should contact him. No, probably not. I mean, perhaps he had the right to know that he was a father but I doubted that he would care. I was certain that mum wouldn't have told him that I was pregnant so it would be a hell of a shock for him if I suddenly rang and told him that he had a daughter. There'd be no point in it anyway. Mum was right about one thing at least: he hadn't wanted me before so why would he want me now?

I looked at Mary and thought of how I would have to be both mother and father to her. That wouldn't be a problem because I had more than enough love to give her. Tim would probably never know it, but I was so grateful to him because he had given me what was, and will always be, the most precious thing in my world.

Later, after the fathers had all gone home, the woman on my right asked about Mary's dad. 'Does he work away, like?' she asked.

'Yes.' It wasn't a lie as such because he did work away in a sense. He certainly didn't work anywhere near where I was.

'He must be happy, though,' she said, 'having a gorgeous little girl like that.'

'Who wouldn't be?' I said, and again it wasn't quite a lie.

She left it at that but I was fairly certain that she didn't believe me. She'd had five children of her own so could probably spot a lie and I doubted that she'd believed what I'd told her. I hadn't actually lied to her though, had I? Not really, I just hadn't told her the truth. Was this how life was going to be from now on? Would I always be hiding my past? I was fairly sure that my mum would be lying to people about what had happened to me and here I was doing just the same.

\*\*\*

Two or three days before I was due to leave hospital, a woman appeared at the door of the ward. She caused a bit of

159

interest because she didn't look like a doctor and it wasn't visiting time. I thought immediately that she had come to see me and I wasn't wrong.

She looked around the room and then came straight to me.

'Susan,' she said, holding out her hand for me to shake. 'I'm Paula.'

'Hello,' I said as she sat down on the chair beside my bed.

As I suspected, Paula had come to talk to me about where Mary and I would be moving on to. My heart was in my mouth, but when she told me that there was an opening at Palmer's Court I allowed myself to breathe.

'I think that you know one of the girls that already live there,' she said.

'Yeah. My best friend Mandy lives there,' I said, surprising myself by how I'd described her. I was happy that we would be living near her.

Paula told me that we would go there when we were discharged from hospital and she explained about the support that I would get once I was there. We would have our own individual flat and be encouraged to live independently but we would have support should we need it.

I knew that things were not going to be easy when we left the hospital. For a start I would be looking after Mary on my own. There wouldn't be nurses on hand to help me when she cried, and that was a bit of a concern to me, but Paula assured me that everyone felt that way and said that I should try not to worry. I had two more days to get as confident as I could before we were on our own and I hoped that would be long enough. Anyway, if I got stuck Mandy would be close by and that made me feel a little better.

'You'll be okay,' Paula said as she stood up to leave. She stroked Mary's tiny fist. 'You'll learn from each other.' She shook my hand again and said that she would see me in two days' time to take me and Mary home.

I liked the sound of that.

The woman in the bed beside me, I think her name might have been Barbara, was flicking through a magazine but I could see that she wasn't really looking at it at all. She was watching Paula leave the ward. Barbara put the magazine down and twisted on her bed so that she was looking at me.

'Everything okay?' she asked.

'Yeah. Fine, thanks.' A feeling of *what the hell* came over me and I decided to come clean. I wasn't ashamed. 'That was a social worker,' I said. 'She came to tell me

161

where Mary and I are going to live when we leave the hospital.'

'Oh!'

Barbara – I am so glad that I finally remembered her name – seemed lost for words.

I would not allow my life, our lives, to become a lie. I didn't want to spend my life hiding my past and why should I? I was proud of my baby.

Barbara was going home the following afternoon; it should have been that afternoon but there had been a problem with her blood pressure or something. 'I'm not complaining though,' she said, after the doctor had told her. 'It means I get another night's rest before I go back to the mad house.' She tried to sound chirpy but she couldn't hide her disappointment. I could understand that; I couldn't wait to leave either. I felt ready for what was coming.

The following morning I watched her getting ready to leave. It would be my turn the following day. Her husband came to collect her and just before she left she came over to my bed where I was sitting on top of the sheets.

'You look after yourself, love,' Barbara said to me and then she looked at Mary, 'and this little one.'

After a final smile just for me she said goodbye to the others and disappeared off the ward with her baby in her

162

arms and her husband close behind. I've often wondered if she changed her mind about having another baby and managed to get the daughter that she longed for.

The following morning, one of the nurses watched as I bathed Mary. I talked to her all the time, Mary that is, calling her pet names, telling her she was a good girl that sort of thing. I did it partly because I liked talking to her but mainly to cover up the fact that I was so nervous. I knew that given practice it would become second nature to me but back then I was terrified.

We'd been ready for nearly an hour when Paula arrived.

'I've come to take you home,' she said and a mad panic came over me. It must have shown in my eyes because she quickly added, 'to your new home.'

For a second I'd thought ... well you know what I'd thought, and Paula did too. She gave me an apologetic smile and rubbed my arm. Once the panic had left me I managed to smile back.

'Ready?' she asked and I nodded my head. She picked up my hospital bag, I picked up my baby and we left the ward.

I know this sounds a bit daft but I'd had this feeling, well more of a fear really that someone was going to come and take Mary away from me. I'd had it since the first time I'd held her and while I know the fear was irrational, it was as though I couldn't believe that I'd be allowed to keep something so precious. Yet here I was, with her in my arms, and we were going home. I knew I was smiling like a lunatic but I didn't care. I was ridiculously happy.

Paula didn't mention it straight away but I wasn't surprised when she asked. 'Have you let your mum know that she's a grandma?' She said it in a matter-of-fact sort of way as we were waiting for a set of traffic lights to change to green. When I didn't answer she looked at me. I only saw her out of the corner of my eye because I was looking at the traffic lights, willing them to change, but they didn't so I was forced to answer her.

I said, 'No,' and left it at that.

She turned her attention back to the road and a few minutes later we pulled up in front of a small block of flats. They looked like three small boxes stacked on top of each other attached to more of the same. There was a patch of grass opposite them and a bit further along I could see a couple of shops. Paula came around to help me and Mary out of the car. 'This is it,' she said. 'I know it's not much to look at, but it's a start. They're quite nice inside.'

*Welcome to Palmer's Court*, I thought to myself. Our flat was number six which meant that it was the second flat up on the left-hand side. Paula said it wasn't ideal because of the pram and everything but there was a lift and if that wasn't working there was a series of walkways that would get you to the ground eventually. I just thought that beggars couldn't be choosers and I'd find a way of dealing with things.

The lift was working that first day and we stood waiting for it to arrive alongside a woman who had a bag of shopping in each hand.

''S'like waiting for Christmas,' she said as she smiled at me. 'You Susan?' she asked.

How did she…? 'Yes,' I said.

The lift arrived and the doors opened. 'Thought so,' she made a gesture with her head that meant we should get in first so we did. I noticed that Paula was smiling. The woman pressed the button marked 2 and as the doors came together she explained. 'Your mate Mandy's my next-door neighbour and she said you'd be moving in today. Who's this then?' She smiled at Mary who was fast sleep in my arms.

'Mary.'

'She's a beauty all right. What number you in?'

'Six,' I told her.

'You're on the same floor as us then,' she said, 'that's good.' The doors opened again and the woman got out. 'Come on, love,' she said, 'you want to be this way.' She stopped outside the first flat that we came to. 'This is you,' she said nodding towards a blue door. She moved her bags in her hand to try and get a better grip. 'I'd shake your hand, love, but you can see how I'm fixed. I'll give Mandy a knock and tell her you've arrived.'

Paula put down the bag that she'd carried from the car and unlocked the door. She opened it and we went inside to a hallway that was about ten feet long. There was a door on the left which went to a bathroom and one on the right that led into the living room. The flat's only bedroom was through a door straight ahead.

'You get yourself settled,' Paula said, 'and I'll put the kettle on.' She went into the living room so I guessed that the kitchen must be attached to that somehow.

The bedroom was bigger than the one that I'd had at ho … at Mum's house. There was a double bed against the middle of one of the smaller walls and a cot to the side of it. There was a wardrobe in one of the corners and a dressing table in the one opposite. Yellow curtains hung from the window, the same shade as the linen that was on the bed and contrasting nicely with the pale blue of the carpet. I liked it.

'I know it's not very big,' Paula startled me when she came up behind me.

166

'No, no, it's fine,' I assured her. 'In fact, it's perfect.' And it was.

As I stood there, in that bedroom, with Mary fast asleep in my arms I felt at peace.

Mind you, the peace was shattered a couple of seconds later by a sharp knock on the front door and a yell of 'Let me in,' through the letter box. We turned to see a pair of eyes looking at us through the slot. It was Mandy. Paula went to open the door and I lay Mary down in her cot. She moved around a little and then settled without even opening her eyes. I felt that she could feel the peace too.

By the time I came out of the bedroom Mandy had parked her pram in the hallway and was standing over it adjusting a blanket. When she saw me she stood up, walked towards me with her arms wide open and wrapped them around me. I wrapped my arms around her too and we stood there hugging each other.

'You stopping for a brew?' Paula asked and when Mandy gave her a look she added, 'Daft question,' and disappeared again.

'You all right?' Mandy asked and all I could do was nod. I didn't trust myself to speak because I was feeling something in my chest that I couldn't understand. It was warm but more than that, it was moving too. I was like happiness was bouncing around inside of me.

We went through to the living room and that was when I saw that the kitchen was a little room that ran off it. The wall opposite the kitchen was made up of one huge window with a glass door that opened on to a small veranda and it made the room light and airy. There was a sofa and one armchair in the room, a television and a small table with one dining chair tucked underneath it. Not a lot, but enough. The sofa had seen better days and was a bit worn on the arms but it was nothing that a throw couldn't hide. Mandy and I sat next to each other on it and when Paula brought the tea through she sat down in the armchair. Mandy and I sat sipping our tea, looking at each other and giggling. We had formed a special bond and it was strong.

'So,' Paula said, 'you settling in all right, Mandy?'

Mandy said that she was. 'You'll like it here,' she said to me. 'I know it's not much to look at but it's OK. And I know it's got a reputation for being a bit rough but that's just people from outside talking. It's all right really. And the good thing is that the old 'uns look after you. I mean, they're not stupid, they know why we're here but they don't judge you. Well they didn't me anyway, apart from that old bag that lives on the bottom in the corner. Miriam soon put her

168

right.' She stopped for breath and a mouthful of tea. 'You met Miriam on the way up. She told me you were here. She's a good old bird is Miriam.'

Mandy always spoke a lot when she was excited and there was no stopping her that day. She told me all about the people that lived on the same landing as us. Apart from me, her and Miriam, there was a man called Bob who hadn't come out of his flat much since he'd broken his leg a few weeks before. Apparently he was on the mend but it would be another few weeks before he got out and about. His daughter came every day to make sure that he was all right and do a bit of shopping for him. Bob lived in the flat next to Miriam and then between Bob and the flat that I'd moved into were Dan and Louise. 'They never had any children of their own,' Mandy said, 'so they like to make a fuss of me and Jade when they see us. I dare say they'll be the same with you. They're away at the minute in Scotland visiting their niece but they'll be back at the weekend.'

I didn't really know about the reputation of Palmer's Court. I'd never heard of it before Sharon had told me that there was a chance that I would be moving there after my baby was born. All I knew was that it was a block of council-owned flats and, from what Mandy had said, I – we – would be all right there.

Paula stayed about an hour or so and before she left she gave me a card that had her telephone number on. 'Any problems, you call me, day or night,' she said. She looked in on Mary who was still asleep in her cot and then peeped into Jade's pram to find that she was showing signs of waking up.

'I'll leave you two to it,' she said and gave us both a hug. 'See you both soon.'

The door had only just closed when Jade did wake up. She gave out a howl that even I with less than a week of experience as a mother could recognise as an *I'm hungry* yell.

Mandy picked her up and gave her to me. 'Hold her will you, while I just heat up her bottle.'

Mandy took a prepared bottle of baby milk from the bag that sat in the basket under the pram and went about warming it up. I rocked Jade but there was no placating her and I wondered what I was doing wrong. It was just one of many moments of self doubt that I would have and I was relieved when Mandy took her off me and started to feed her. Jade sucked hard on the bottle and made contented little snorting noises as her stomach started to fill.

'There's a bottle made up in the fridge for Mary,' Mandy said, 'and if you want my advice, you'll make another one up as soon as one's gone. You don't want to have to do it when the little un's bawling the place down.' Motherhood suited Mandy.

I decided to leave them alone and went to look around my new home. In the kitchen there was a gas cooker, with a selection of saucepans sitting on top of the rings, a fridge and an automatic washing machine. I opened the fridge and inside it there was a bottle of milk, a small block of cheese, a packet of ham, a chicken leg and a bag of carrots. The bottle of baby formula that Mandy had mentioned sat in the door section. I closed the fridge and checked the cupboards. There were tea bags, a jar of coffee and about a dozen tins of various things including baked beans and tuna. I'd manage that day but I'd need to do some shopping. On the bench, in the corner just by the window that looked out onto the landing that we had walked along, was a steriliser with several bottles inside it and a tin of formula.

Everything I needed was in that flat, including my baby and my best friend.

When I went back into the living room Jade had finished her bottle and was sitting forward on her mum's knee having her back rubbed. Mandy was encouraging her and when she finally did let out an enormous burp Mandy said, 'Good girl! Better out than in,' and we both laughed.

171

Mary woke up to be fed not long after that so Mandy said that she would get off but that she'd be back in the morning to take me shopping. 'If it's anything like when I arrived,' she said, 'you'll be okay for the first night but then you'll need to get something in. We'll need to go to the post office first though,' she said as she was leaving, 'so that you can get your money.'

That was the one thing that I didn't like about the situation that I was in: the money; the handouts that I would have to live on. Mum had had a word for people that lived on 'the social' and it wasn't nice. But hey, I'd have to get used to it; there was no choice and I had no place for pride where Mary was concerned. I was willing to do whatever it took to bring her up. My mum had something bad to say about everyone that didn't live by her own moral standards, so God knows what she'd be saying about me now.

I was still thinking about that as I sat on the sofa with a cushion supporting my back and my baby in my arms. Mary was flicking the teat of the bottle I was offering her around with her tongue until finally she managed to get it where she wanted it and started to suck. I loved her so much but I was fully aware of what I had given up to be there with her. No matter what Mum said, I had known what I was doing when I decided to have her. I'd known that life wouldn't be a bed

172

of roses, but I was willing to risk it. And I have never – not for one second – regretted running away so that I could keep her.

Maybe, if I had stayed, Mum would have fallen in love with her when she was born and allowed me to keep her but somehow I doubted it. In Mum's eyes, Mary was the embodiment of shame and she wouldn't have that in the house. Running away had been my only choice and I would have done it again in a heart beat.

I couldn't help wondering how Mum was covering up the fact that I wasn't around. At least one of the neighbours would have mentioned it by now. Mrs Watson who lived in the house opposite us was what Mum called 'a curtain twitcher' and there wasn't a lot went on in that street that she didn't know about. She was bound to have noticed that I hadn't been around and she would have asked about me. She probably hadn't asked directly because she never did that, but she would have made it her business to find out what was going on.

Later that night, when Mary was bathed, fed and fast asleep in her cot I sat on my threadbare sofa and looked through the large window. It was pitch black outside and the lights from the town beyond Palmer's Court twinkled. Even though I'd told myself to stop thinking about it, or rather her,

I couldn't help myself. Paula had asked if I had contacted her and I was glad that she hadn't pressed the point but as I sat alone I wondered if maybe I should give her a ring or at least write her a letter. Maybe I should have, but the truth was that I didn't want to. It's like I've said: to my mum, Mary would just be something to be ashamed of, a dirty little secret that should be hidden away and there was no way I was going to let her become that.

At the end of the day though, she was still my mum and despite everything I still yearned for her love. I've loved her all my life and you don't just stop loving someone because they do something that you don't agree with. But I loved Mary more and if I had to choose one of them I would choose Mary every day. And though I loved Mum, I didn't think I could forgive her and I doubted she would ever be able to accept my decision. What the neighbours thought would always come first, it was just the way she was. Julie had told me that and she was right. So I definitely wasn't going to contact my mum, but what about Julie?

I assumed that Julie had got the letter that I'd sent before I left and from the bottom of my heart I wanted to get in touch with her. I wanted to tell her all about her beautiful niece. I would have to ring her; a letter would give them a clue as to where I was and I knew that I didn't want that. Maybe I would ring her the next day.

'You sure you want to do that?' Mandy asked me the next morning when I told her about my plan. She'd come round after breakfast so that we could go shopping together and she sat on the end of my bed while I finished getting Mary dressed.

'Yes, I think so.' Mary had a white babygro on and kicked her feet as I tried to fasten the buttons.

'Will she tell your sister where you are?'

'I'm not going to tell her where I am, just that she has a niece and that we are all right.'

And that's what I did. As Mandy sat on the bench with a pram either side of her I stood in the phone box and dialled Julie's number. It rang five or six times and I started to think that she must be out. Maybe I'd wait until after six; she'd definitely be home then and it would be cheaper so I'd get more minutes for my money. I almost put the phone down but decided to count five more rings before I gave up. She answered on ring number four.

'Hello?' she said. I didn't speak straight away. I opened my mouth but nothing came out. 'Hello,' she said again and still nothing came out. And then she said something that took me totally by surprise. 'Susan,' she said, 'is that you?'

'Yes,' finally a word popped out.

'Oh my God, Susan! Where are you?' she asked. 'How are you?'

'I'm fine,' I said. I could hear my voice shaking and I took a deep breath. 'I'm fine,' I said again. 'We're fine.'

'We? Did you have the baby?'

'Yes. You have a niece, Julie. A beautiful, little niece.'

I thought I heard Julie crying. 'Are you both okay? What did you call her? Are you coming back?' It was just one question after another without a wait for an answer.

'Yes, we are both fine,' I said. 'Her name is Mary and no we are not coming back.'

'Why not? There's nothing she can do now.'

I gave a little laugh. I couldn't help it. 'Oh come on, Julie,' I said. 'I don't know what she's told the neighbours but whatever it is I'm sure me turning up with Mary in my arms would put a spanner in the works. What has she told the neighbours anyway?'

'That you're in Scarborough looking after Dad's auntie Rose.'

So now I knew. 'I just wanted you to know that I was safe,' I said emphasising the word 'you'.

'Thanks for that. I appreciate it. I've been worried about you.' She paused for a couple of seconds before asking, 'Do you want me to tell her that you rang?'

'Do you think she'll care?'

The pips got in the way of her answer.

'Call again,' she said before we got cut off.

I didn't know if I would.

***

Miriam knocked on my door one day at the beginning of December. It was one of those really bright days that are freezing despite the sun's best efforts. I opened the door wide and told her to come in.

'I thought I'd seen Mandy come in,' she said, 'so I'd thought I'd catch you both together.'

'She's through there.' I nodded towards the living room and closed the door.

'You all right, Miriam?' Mandy said. 'Sorry if Jade's been keeping you up. The doctor says its colic and he's given me some medicine for her.'

'Is that why you think I'm here?' Miriam laughed. 'To complain about babies crying? Babies crying don't bother me. One of the benefits of being deaf in one ear, I suppose. Can't hear a thing once I'm laid on it.' She sat down in the armchair and asked, 'Are we having a brew?'

They were talking about colic when I came back with the tea and Miriam took a sip of hers before she told us why she had wanted to catch us together.

'It's about Christmas,' Miriam said. 'I wondered what you were both doing.'

I can't say I'd given it a lot of thought, mainly because it was something that I didn't want to think about. I loved Christmas, and say what you like about my mother she knew how to roast a turkey; I was going to miss that – not the food as such but the family time.

Mandy and I both said that we hadn't thought about it.

'Just as well I have then, isn't it,' Miriam said. 'You'll come to me.'

'We couldn't…' Mandy and I both started to say.

'Oh, but you could and you will,' Miriam said. 'All four of you.'

So that's what we did.

\*\*\*

'Merry Christmas,' Miriam said a few weeks later as she opened the door to us. She was wearing a red apron that matched the colour of her face and I couldn't help wondering if she'd been hitting the sherry already. She made us feel so welcome that day, and I well up every time I think about it now.

There was a small, artificial tree full of baubles and lights sitting in the corner of Miriam's living room and tinsel was wrapped around the pictures on the wall. Under the tree there were presents for both of us as well as our children. Just small things, bubble bath for Mandy and me and a small teddy each for the girls, but it's the thought that counts and the memory of that thought has never left me. I had never known such kindness. Mandy and I had clubbed together and bought Miriam a matching hat and scarf set which she said she loved and I used to see her wearing it so I think she really did.

Miriam had said that she would buy the turkey and Mandy and I bought the vegetables, well the sprouts and the carrots because that was all we could afford. 'Meat and two veg,' Miriam said, 'that's more than enough for anyone.' She'd bought a small Christmas pudding and made her own custard which was the closest thing to heaven on a plate that I have ever tasted.

After lunch, as the babies slept in their prams, we sat with Miriam, drank tea and watched some film on the television. It was a musical I think. I didn't really pay much attention to it if I'm honest I was just enjoying being happy.

Later when we were home and Mary was tucked up in bed I stood by the big window and looked out into the darkness. I thought about how things had been last Christmas Day. I'd gone out with Tim in the evening and we'd exchanged gifts in The Flying Horse. I'd bought him some aftershave that I couldn't really afford and he gave me a box of talc. Note I said gave and not bought because there was a good chance that he'd nicked it. Things were very different now.

***

I bought myself a card that first Mother's Day. I know that sounds silly, a bit pathetic even, but I just wanted to mark the occasion. It was just a small one, white with pink edges and a picture of a sleeping baby on it. 'On Your First Mother's Day' was written along the top. I would never have another first Mother's Day and it didn't matter to me that I'd bought the card myself. I didn't write on it, I just stood it on the table and looked at it. I kept it of course; I've still got it now, tucked inside the shoe box under my bed. The card's a bit yellow now where it used to be white and the writing is faded.

Mandy laughed at me and called me 'soppy cow' when she saw it. I shrugged my shoulders and couldn't disagree with her.

I didn't celebrate my birthday that year. I spent my nineteenth birthday dusting shelves and vacuuming carpets just like I did every other day. My only concession to it being any different to every other day of the year was that I made a cake. It wasn't much of a cake, just a Victoria sponge but it was the first birthday cake I'd ever had in my life. That made me feel sad and I vowed that day that Mary would always have a cake on her birthday.

Mandy came round that afternoon, as she did most days, and I gave her a piece to have with her tea. 'What's the occasion?' she asked.

'Just felt like baking,' I said and I don't know why I didn't tell her it was my birthday.

Occasions, family times like birthdays, were always a bit tough. They were the times that I missed my ... people the most.

But never mind, being with Mary was worth it.

***

Life settled down and Mary and I found a way of getting along together. We did all right most of the time. I mean, there was the odd occasion in those early days when I would have given anything for a good night's sleep, or even half a night's sleep, but apart from that we got along fine.

'Maybe you would do better if you had help from your family,' the snooty health visitor had said to me one day when I took Mary to the clinic to get checked out.

I didn't know where she'd come from, she wasn't local though because she had a really posh accent, and I mean *really* posh. Knowing what I know now, I think it was probably Surrey or somewhere like that. Not London but definitely that way on. And you just knew that she'd come from a good family where the sort of thing that she had to deal with in her job day to day never happened. She hadn't got a clue what life was like for people like me. Mandy had had more than one run in with her.

That wasn't my way though, so when she suggested again that I needed the support of my family I politely said that wasn't possible and thank goodness she didn't press it because I think I might have told her that they were all dead just to shut her up. I felt terrible about that later because that was the sort of thing that you didn't joke about.

Then it occurred to me that they could die and I wouldn't know about it. My family had no way of contacting me to let me know. But by that same token I could die too, so I guessed it was a two-way street. Anyway, Mary was my family now, my real family. But do you know what, no matter how many times I said that to myself, I couldn't help thinking about the one that I had left behind.

It was sunny that day so instead of going straight back up to the flat after my appointment with the health visitor, I sat on the bench on the grassy area. Mary was fast asleep in her pram so I positioned her so that the sun wasn't in her face, sat back and relaxed.

I could see my flat from where I sat and something about it made me think of egg boxes stacked on top of each other. Whenever I think of that flat now I always think of egg boxes.

Egg box or not, I loved that flat. It wasn't much but it was mine and a palace couldn't have been more precious. Mandy and I had come across a charity shop in town where we could buy bits and bobs for our flats, our babies and even sometimes ourselves, though that was a rarity in my case. This was in the days before charity shops became fashionable and most people wouldn't have been seen dead walking into one. We used to watch them sometimes looking up and down the street to make sure that no one they knew was going to see them before making a dash for the door. We used to laugh because we couldn't understand it. You could get good stuff in there at a reasonable price. So what if it had been used before?

Anyway, like I say, we found this charity shop and I used to buy stuff for the flat. That, plus that fact that I polished the place until it shone like a new pin meant that it didn't look half bad.

Paula commented on it one day when she came round for one of her regular visits. 'You've got the place looking really good,' she said, looking at the throw that covered the balding patch on the sofa and the couple of new, similarly coloured cushions that tied it all together. 'You've done a great job.'

I'll admit it, I felt proud that someone thought that I kept a nice house but I tried to shake the feeling away because that was a road I did not want to go down.

I'm not going to pretend that life was easy because to be honest it was anything but. I've already mentioned the sleepless nights and on top of that there was the loneliness. I had Mandy, who was great – she was such a support – and there was Paula who came to see me on a regular basis, but neither of them was there in the middle of the night. Once I'd locked the door that was it; just me and Mary and, love her as I did, she wasn't a lot of company.

For the first few months I was terrified every time she cried during the night. What would I do if there was anything seriously wrong with her? The nearest phone was out the door down the steps and across the courtyard. Anyway, who would I ring? I may have had help from my friend and my social worker but ultimately I was alone and that got to me sometimes, especially in the early days. I cried a lot of tears.

184

But somehow I got through them, we got through them together. As the months passed Mary found her ways of communicating with me and I somehow managed to understand her. We made a good team.

There wasn't a lot of money for food, so once Mary progressed to solid food I tried to make meals that I could mash down for her to eat. It was cheaper than the jars from the shop and surely they were better for her. I remember eating a lot of vegetable soup which I would have for my lunch and then, a few hours later when it was cool enough give to Mary to eat once I bashed the veggies to within an inch of their lives. I thanked God that I'd always enjoyed Mrs Clough's Home Economics class at school so at least I was able to cook. I'd make a big saucepan of soup that would last me a few days for just a few pennies.

We used to go food shopping as close to the end of the day as we could, when the fresh stuff was at its cheapest. Mandy taught me that trick; she said it was something that her mother had always done. She was surprised when I'd told her that mine hadn't done the same.

'No,' I told her one day as we were sitting in her flat with the girls playing together on the floor in front of us, 'Mum would never do that.' She looked surprised, so I explained. 'She'd never do that because it would be a sign that she was struggling to cope, you know, with money. You can't have the neighbours thinking that you're hard up.'

Mandy just shook her head, 'I'll never understand your mother,' she said.

That made two of us.

Mary took her first step when she was about ten months old. She'd been wobbling around, hanging on to the few bits of furniture for a few weeks and then one day she just went. I mean it was only a couple of steps before she bounced down onto her padded bottom but I was so excited. I just wanted to tell someone but when I looked around there was no one there to share the moment with.

'Clever girl, Mary,' I said grabbing hold of the tiny hands that she was holding out to me. She pulled herself up, got her balance and then walked into my arms. We hugged each other and I think I probably cried.

I told anyone who would listen that she'd walked. When I was cleaning the kitchen windows I saw Bob coming out of his front door. 'Guess what?' I shouted, 'Mary walked.'

She learned to talk pretty quickly as well and before her second birthday she was putting simple sentences together. The old health visitor that I'd had when Mary was born, the posh one, had retired when Mary was about six months old

186

and been replaced by a younger woman who had just left university and was full of new ideas.

'Talk to her all the time,' she'd said, 'doesn't matter what about, just talk to her.'

So I did and it paid off.

We were moved from Palmer's Court when Mary was about two and a half. Paula said that a one bedroom flat was no longer suitable for us now that Mary was getting older. She said that Mary would need a room of her own. I was sad to leave that flat but I knew that Paula was probably right. We were moved to a two-bedroom house about half a mile away.

Number 11 Nightingale Terrace had a living room and kitchen downstairs and upstairs was a biggish bedroom at the front, a smaller one at the back and a bathroom in between. It reminded me a lot of the house that I'd grown up in except for the enclosed yard at the back. The house I'd grown up in had had a long garden. I had a garden at the front though, just a small one.

Mandy had also moved out of Palmer's Court for the same reason. We no longer lived a few doors away from each other though we were only separated by a few streets so I still got to see her almost every day.

I think the girls would have been coming up to three when Mandy met Daniel. She asked me if I'd babysit Jade while she went out with him one night. Of course I said I would because Mary and Jade got along so well and why shouldn't at least one of us be having a bit of fun? I know that makes me sound bitter but I'm not really. Well, maybe a little bit...

Anyway, Mandy had met Daniel and the one night babysitting turned into another and then another one. She seemed serious about him. That was until she turned up at my house one night about ten o'clock crying her eyes out. I almost bounced to the door. Who the hell was banging on it like that so late at night? They'd wake the children. The door was on a chain and I opened it a crack to see who it was and when I saw Mandy there with tears streaming down her face I opened it as quickly as I could and dragged her inside.

We stayed up talking for hours that night and she never did tell me exactly what had happened. Suffice to say that she didn't ask me to babysit again for a long time.

The thought of a boyfriend terrified me. I mean, look how the last one had turned out. When I looked at Mary she seemed worth all the heartache. I had her now; I didn't need a man. Like I've said, I was lonely sometimes but I just didn't feel like I could open myself up to that type of rejection again.

I thought about Tim from time to time, wondered how he was and what he was up to. Sometimes, especially when I was struggling to make ends meet, I thought that maybe I'd been wrong to keep Mary from him. Shouldn't he have been forced to shoulder some of the responsibility too? But it was enough that he had rejected me without him rejecting her too. And anyway, I could hardly turn up after all this time and say, 'Oh, by the way, this is your daughter,' could I? I somehow didn't see him dancing a jig at the prospect of fatherhood.

The thought of a man, any man, scared me.

That was until I met Joe.

I met Joe in the library. I loved to read but money being as tight as it was I couldn't afford to buy books, not even ones from the charity shop. Every other Monday I would go to the library in the afternoon to pick up a couple of books for myself and a couple from the junior section for Mary. Mandy used to have both girls for a couple of hours so that I could browse the books in peace and I would return the favour if Mandy every needed a bit of 'me' time.

Anyway I'd seen Joe in the library a couple of times. I hadn't really paid him a lot of attention, just noticed him really, like I had the bald fella with the glasses; just noticed him. So, he came over to me one day and said that he'd noticed me too and he wondered if I fancied going out some time for a drink. I hadn't had a bloke take the slightest bit of interest in me since Tim so it came as a bit of a surprise, but I mumbled something and we got chatting. He asked if he could see me the following night for a drink and I thought *why the hell not*? So it was agreed.

''Course I will,' Mandy said when I asked her if she'd have Mary.

It had been over three years since my last date and I was as nervous as I had been that first time. I had taken Mary over to Mandy's house on the inaptly named Starling Avenue earlier in the afternoon and I had the house all to myself. I didn't like it.

Joe was already in the pub when I got there. He waved me over and asked me what I wanted to drink. I settled for an orange juice; somehow I'd lived for over twenty years and never once tasted alcohol so, when he asked if I was sure that was all I wanted, I said yes.

Okay, so I'm going to cut a short story even shorter here: it didn't work out. We had a couple of drinks and chatted and as we did it became clear that he had certain 'expectations' of how the night would end and I'm sure that

I don't have to spell that out for you. When I twigged what his intentions were I made it clear that he was going to be disappointed.

'Why?' he asked as he slurped another mouthful of beer. 'It's not like you're saving yourself for your wedding night or anything is it?' And just in case I hadn't understood his meaning he added, 'Well, you've got a baby haven't you?'

Well that was the end of that. I was no longer the naïve kid that I'd once been and I realised that I was no longer scared of a man rejecting me because he couldn't get his way. I wouldn't be sleeping with anyone, thank you very much. I told him as much, bid him goodnight, thanked him for the drinks and left without a backward glance. I changed the day that I went to the library and I never saw him again.

After I'd left the pub I didn't want to go home to an empty house so I went to Mandy's. She seemed surprised to see me but not by the story that I told her. I didn't want to get Mary out of her warm bed and I didn't want to go home alone so I spent the night on Mandy's sofa, but not before we'd stayed up talking well into the early hours.

\*\*\*

Mary started nursery just after her fourth birthday. I was sorry to be without her but I knew that it would do her good and to be honest she was ready for it. She got a place in the morning session and Jade, who had started the term before, was on the afternoon one. I was a bit worried about that at first. I mean, Mary was going to be doing something all on her own for the first time in her life but as it turned out it was probably a good thing because she was forced to make new friends. Unlike me when I was young, she made friends very easily and settled into nursery life without any trouble.

A year later I cried when I saw her dressed in a little grey pinafore dress, a white shirt and a green cardigan. Mary was ready for her first day at school. I couldn't say the same for myself.

## JEAN

Mick never spoke about Susan, not to me anyway but I knew he thought about her. I used to watch him sitting in the chair looking off into space and I knew what he doing. He'd once said to me that he knew me but there was no one in the world knew him better than I did. I knew him better than he knew himself. He was thinking about her all right but he never talked about her.

But whether we talked about it or not, I knew that Susan was past her time. I knew that she would have her baby – or not – by now. Well, I'm just saying. How did I know? Anything could have happened.

Anything could have happened to my baby and I didn't know. I'm not heartless you know; Susan was my baby and I cared about her but she had made her choice. She'd chosen the illegitimate baby of a man that didn't want her over us, her family. That's gratitude for you.

Anyway, I used to wonder about her and the baby. What she'd had, had it been bad for her things like that and then one day Julie came to visit and said, 'Susan phoned.'

193

'What?' Mick nearly choked on the food he was eating –
steak and kidney pie as I recall – well, more kidney than
steak, I mean, we didn't have money to burn. Funny the
things that you remember. Anyway, after Julie's
announcement he put his knife and fork down and so did I.

Julie sat down at the table with us and she looked at each
of us in turn but I noticed she was looking at her dad when
she said, 'Susan phoned,' again.

'What did she say?' he asked. There was more life in his
voice than I'd heard for months. 'How is she?'

'She's fine.'

He'd grabbed Julie's hand and she put her other hand on
top of his. It was like I wasn't even there.

Julie said that Susan had told her she'd had a baby girl
and called her Mary. She told us that Susan had said that
they were both all right. Mick asked her to go over it again,
what had Susan said exactly? She repeated it but nothing
changed from the first time. He was hanging on to every
word she said.

'Did you ask her where she was?' he asked.

'Yes.'

'Did she tell you?'

'No.'

He nodded his head slowly, patted Julie's hands and said. 'She's all right and that's the main thing.' He pushed himself up from the table. 'And she'll be looking after that baby,' he added as he disappeared towards the living room.

We both watched him leave but neither of us followed him.

I asked Julie if that was really all that Susan had said and she nodded her head but I knew that she was lying. I don't know why they bothered; they should just have told me the truth straight away. 'Really?' was all I needed to say.

'I asked her why she wasn't coming back and she basically said that she didn't want to upset the apple cart.' She paused for a second or two, like she was letting me take in what she had just told me before she carried on. 'She said that she didn't know what you'd told the neighbours but she thought her coming back with a baby would cause a problem for you. "Put a spanner in the works" is what she said, I think.'

Well she wasn't wrong there, but I didn't say anything.

Julie didn't stay long after that and when she'd gone I sat where I was at the table.

So Susan had a daughter, we had a granddaughter. Part of me wished that I could celebrate it. I wished that I could accept her baby and what had happened but I couldn't. I'd wanted certain things for Susan: A levels, maybe even a degree. Putting her through university would have been hard but it would have been worth it. She wasn't stupid, she could have done something with her life and now she'd gone and thrown it all away. She'd shown herself to be no better than any number of lasses on this estate that got themselves pregnant by lads that were no good. And the one thing that I hadn't wanted for my girls: she'd shown that she was no better than me.

I was sure that Susan thought she loved her baby – she probably thought that Mary was the best thing in the world – but it would just be a matter of time before she started resenting the child for holding her back. She wouldn't be able to do the things that she wanted to do, go to the places that she wanted to go to, not with a baby to think about. How long would it be before she realised that I actually knew what I was talking about? Not that she'd ever admit it; she was too stubborn for that, too much like Mick's mother, but that stubbornness would do her no favours. That was the real reason that she couldn't come home. It wasn't that she was afraid of 'upsetting the apple cart' or whatever she'd said to Julie; she just wouldn't be able to bring herself to admit that I'd been right.

I was there ages and by the time that I finally moved myself and started washing the dishes, the gravy had set like cement on the plates.

I was scrubbing at a plate when I felt Mick looking at me. I could just sense that he was there. I hadn't heard him come in, so I had no idea how long he'd been watching me.

'Mary,' he said eventually, 'where do you think that came from?'

There was something in his voice, something not *kind* exactly but softer than it had been for months.

'I don't know,' I said in answer to his question.

Mick changed that night. He wasn't back to his old self but he seemed more at peace. He was at least able to bring himself to speak to me a bit more often, so our home situation became more bearable.

***

'Your Susan not coming home for Christmas?' Ida Watson had caught me in the street on my way back from the post office a couple of days after Susan had phoned Julie.

'No,' I told her. 'It's like I said, Ida, she likes it over there. She's settled and she's got new friends.' I tried to move away but she wasn't going to let me get away that lightly. Why would she? I'd have been the same in her shoes.

197

'Even so, I thought she might come home for Christmas.'

'Yes, well, she's not.' I was sharper than I'd meant to be but I knew what Ida was getting at. And, what's more, she knew that I knew. 'She was on the phone the other day and she's fine,' I said. 'That's all I need to know.'

'Can't live their lives for them, can we?' she said, with a look on her face. She might have claimed it was a smile but it looked more like a smirk to me.

It was nearly Christmas though and Susan was out there somewhere with her baby. Under different circumstances I would have enjoyed looking for things for a granddaughter. I'd have bought her little fairy frocks and teddy bears galore. I've never told this to anyone this but I did buy a teddy bear for her, as a Christmas present. Stupid, I know, because who knew if I would ever get the chance to give it to her? But I did it anyway. It was a caramel colour with a pink ribbon around its neck. It's still wrapped up in Christmas paper in the bottom of my wardrobe. God knows what they'll think when they're going through my stuff after I'm gone.

I spent a lot of time thinking about Susan on Christmas Day and I know I wasn't the only one. It was heartbreaking really because I think Mick was hoping she would come home. It would have been the best Christmas present he could ever have had but in his heart he knew he wouldn't get it.

'I thought she might have rung,' I said, as me and Julie were clearing the dishes away after Christmas Dinner. Mick and Chris had left us to it.

Julie didn't say anything; she just piled dishes on top of each other and took them to the sink. I watched her as she rested the plates on the tiny little bump that was starting to form on her belly. I had never seen her look happier, or healthier for that matter than she had since she found out she was pregnant.

Sadly for everyone though, Julie only got to enjoy the feeling for another few months. She was twenty-two weeks gone when she woke in the middle of the night in a pool of blood and by the time she got to hospital it was too late. The baby was dead.

'You're young,' I told her when I visited her a few days after it had happened, 'you can try again.' She looked at me as if she couldn't believe what I was saying.

'But it won't be this baby will it, Mum?' she said. 'This baby is dead.'

'Why, Mum? Why?' she asked over and over again and I didn't know what to say to her.

'It just happens sometimes,' I said.

199

'It didn't happen to Helen,' she had tears pouring down her face, 'and it didn't happen to Susan.'

God help me, but I did wonder why it couldn't have happened to Susan.

'Your turn will come,' I told her and I hoped that I was right.

If anything, losing the baby brought Julie and Christopher closer together. I mean, it had always been obvious that Christopher adored her but after the baby he was just so careful with her. He cared for her, not in a sickly, over the top sort of way but – I don't know how I'd put it really – it was just obvious that she was the most special person in the world to him. I hoped she realised just how lucky she was.

But while they were more in love than ever, the same couldn't be said for Helen and Robert. Like I've said, we didn't see as much of them as we did Julie and Chris but when we did, it was clear that something was going wrong between them. Helen didn't say anything, not at first anyway but I'm her mother and I could see her pain. At first I just thought that they'd had a row. I mean, even the happiest of couples have rows, but when things were still the same when they came around the week before my birthday I asked her if she was all right.

'Just got a headache,' she said, but she was as bad as Julie at lying so I knew that her head was fine. I don't think Robert spoke to her once while they were there. He talked about football with Mick and he played with James a bit but he totally ignored his wife. James was getting on for three by then and so far there'd been no sign of any more babies. From the look of things, there wouldn't be any more any time soon.

'Was Robert all right?' I asked Mick after they'd gone home.

'Yeah, he was fine. Not very happy with United's result yesterday but who was?'

What was it about men and football?

'Did you talk about anything else?'

'No.'

Maybe I was imagining it. Maybe Helen had just had a headache but I didn't think so.

A couple of months later, Robert was back at his mother's and Helen was crying her heart out on the telephone. Turned out that Robert had met someone through work and he'd been seeing her on a regular basis since before Christmas. Helen had had her suspicions for a while but hadn't said anything. I suppose she hadn't wanted to believe it was true. Who would? No woman wants to think that they aren't enough for their husband. But they were rowing about something one day and in her temper she'd asked him about it. He'd denied it at first – well, he would wouldn't he – but eventually he'd admitted it. I don't know if she threw him out or if he left of his own accord but either way he was back at his mother's.

'Don't worry love,' I told her. 'He'll be back before you know it.' I don't think she believed me and, to be honest, I don't know if I believed myself. There'd always been something about Robert that I wasn't sure about. He looked down his nose at all of us, including Helen, sometimes. That used to annoy the life out of me but I hadn't said anything because he was her choice. I don't suppose you should blame him for it; it was the way he'd been brought up. They'd always thought that they were better than anyone else because they lived on the better end of the estate and Robert's dad wore a suit to work. He only sold insurance for God's sake.

As the weeks passed there was no sign of him coming home. I rang Helen every day and her dad went to her house regularly just to check on her and James. The baby was too young to know what was going on but Helen was a mess.

I didn't normally go round to Helen's or Julie's without being invited because I'd never wanted to be accused of being an interfering mother-in-law, but now Robert wasn't there that didn't apply any more. And thank God I did go. Helen looked terrible. I know she wasn't wearing any make-up but my God she was pale, and you could have carried potatoes in the bags under her eyes. My heart was breaking at the sight of her and I think if I could have got my hands on Robert I would have wrung his neck for what he was doing to my daughter.

I held her as she cried, something I hadn't done since she was a very little girl. Helen rarely let her emotions show so the fact that she was allowing me to cradle her while she sobbed told me just how low she was.

'Why, Mum?' she asked and there was no answer to that one either.

By the time I went home she was calm again. She said that she didn't think she had any more tears to cry but I thought she probably wrong about that. I made her something to eat before I left because by the look of her she hadn't seen food for a while. She'd never had much weight about her but by then she was stick thin. I told her that she had to keep her strength up for James' sake if not for her own and she promised that she would eat the food I'd made

203

later. She said that she might even open a bottle of wine but I didn't think that was a good idea. Before I left I gave her a big hug; it just felt like the right thing to do.

Later, as I sat on my own, I thought about what had happened that afternoon. Mick had gone out for a drink and I sat in the armchair trying to watch something on the television but I couldn't get into it because I couldn't stop thinking about Helen and what had happened between us. I've probably already said that I've never been a touchy-feely sort of person but that afternoon when Helen needed me to be one I had been. I'd held her and comforted her and been there for her.

Perhaps if I'd been able to do the same for Susan, she wouldn't have disappeared. I knew that I hadn't been the mother she'd wanted me to be, but I'd done what I thought was best for her. I had been a good mother to her; I'd given her the best advice I could. I hadn't been able to see any way she could possibly have had the baby and raised it on her own without ruining her life and I would never in a million years have told her that she should marry Tim Preston. Susan would never have been happy with him and she would have been miserable all her life rather than admit she'd made a mistake. Why would I want that for her?

Oh my God I had made such a mess of things.

I was still sitting in the chair when Mick came in. I hadn't heard him come through the back door and I hadn't seen him come through the living room door, but suddenly he was just there.

'What's wrong?' he asked. 'It's not Helen is it? He hasn't come round and done anything to her has he?'

'No, it's not Helen.'

'What is it then?'

'I've just been thinking.' There was something that I needed to get off my chest. 'Sit down a minute, Mick,' I said. He sat on the end of the sofa about two feet away from me. It was now or never. 'I've been thinking about Susan.' I took a few seconds to work out what it was that I wanted to say. 'I did what I did because I thought it was the best for her. For her,' I emphasised that bit, 'do you understand that? I know you all think that I did it because I was worried about what the neighbours would think and maybe I was in part – I mean, I'll admit that I didn't want the shame of it – but I suggested adoption because I didn't want her throwing her life away. And she would have been throwing her life away; you know that, Mick, especially if she'd tied herself to that bloody Preston lad. I mean that little lad that Mary Dobson's daughter's had is his, not that he's having anything to do with either of them. He's moved on to his next victim now.'

'But was adoption the only way, Jean?' For a second it looked like he was going to move his hand towards me but he didn't.

'I thought it was and I thought her going to Scarborough was the best way to go about it. That way nobody round here would have known about it. You know how they would have talked and she would have hated that.' I don't know if he realised that he was nodding his head just ever so slightly. 'I thought that she could have the baby adopted and then come back and pick up her life again.'

'As if nothing had happened?' He stopped nodding and looked at me. 'Did you not know her at all?' He wasn't being cruel, he was just pointing out a truth that I had only just realised.

'Not as well as I thought.' And then I finally plucked up the courage to ask a question that had been on my mind for a long time. 'Did you really see her the night she ran away?' I looked at him and defied him to lie to me. He didn't answer me straight away.

'No,' he said eventually but I didn't know if he was telling me the truth.

'We've got a granddaughter Mick, a granddaughter that we've never seen and it's all my fault.'

He didn't disagree with me.

'A granddaughter that we might never see. And all those things that I was worried about for Susan – you know, her being stuck on her own with a baby, her not having the life I wanted for her – well, she's got that life now.' I whispered the next words, 'Except now she's doing it completely alone.' I hadn't been sure that I would say this next bit but, that night, words were just falling out of my mouth. 'I was wondering ... do you think we should try looking for her?'

'Where would we start?' he asked.

He had a point. Susan had been gone for the best part of a year and we'd only had the letter she'd sent the night she went and one phone call from her and God knows where she'd been ringing from. This was long before the days of caller recognition so unless you were the police you had no way of telling where someone was ringing from. I thought of suggesting that we go to the police but like I've just said, she'd been gone for almost a year, she was nearly nineteen years old and she had said in a letter that she didn't want to be found. They wouldn't do anything. It would be down to us. Mick was right though, where would we start?

'She'll be back one day,' he said and I looked at him.

'Do you really think so?' I wanted to believe him because I wanted to get the chance to tell her that I was sorry: sorry that I'd let her down, sorry for not being there for her when she needed me.

Mick nodded his head. 'Family is important to Susan, and no matter what, we are still family. I'd bet my life that she'll be back one day.'

I hoped that he was right and that I would live long enough to see that day.

***

To get to the day that I hoped I would see there were a lot of other, ordinary days that we had to get through.

Helen eventually pulled herself together a bit, though she could still be fragile, especially if it was after a day that Robert had been to see James. She never admitted it but I know her and she was hoping that one day when he turned up to see his son he'd arrive with a suitcase in his hand and say that he was coming home. But that never happened and she was left disappointed.

I saw Robert's mother in the supermarket one day a year or two later and it must have been at about three because it was just starting to go dark. She was in the queue at the till and didn't know that I was behind her. I daresay if she had known I was there she wouldn't have been talking about

208

Robert and Becky this and Robert and Becky that. I ignored it for a minute or two but when I heard her telling the assistant 'Robert and Becky are coming to us for Christmas,' I just flipped.

I laughed out loud and the three people between me and her all turned round and looked at me. So did she.

'Sorry,' I said to her but making sure that everyone heard me, 'I couldn't help overhearing you about Robert and his slapper coming to you for Christmas. Do you think he might have a minute to at least give his wife a ring and wish his little boy merry Christmas?' I glared at her. 'Because he couldn't find the time last year.'

I could have kicked myself for making a show like that but my blood was boiling and I hadn't been able to help myself. I'd managed to shut her up though so maybe it was worth it.

By the following Christmas Robert had started divorce proceedings. Apparently Becky was having a baby and they wanted to get married. I was so disappointed when I heard about it, though I should have seen it coming. I'd had such high hopes for her when they got married. All right I know I couldn't stand his mother but it had been a good marriage for her; she had moved up in the world. Now she was going to be a divorcee. I hate that word.

209

By that time, though, the fight had gone out of Helen and she didn't contest it. She said that she just wanted to get it over with. Though she'd never told me herself I knew that Julie had done some babysitting for her while she went out so I wondered if she had met someone herself. If she had, nothing came of it. It was like I'd tried to tell Susan: it was hard for a man to take on another man's child.

That was until she met Richard six months after her divorce was finalised. He was a bit older than her and, like her, was divorced and had a couple of kids of his own but he was a nice enough bloke and he treated her well. More importantly though, he loved James and James loved him. The poor little fella was a bit confused, what with having two sets of parents, but we all just made him feel that he was loved and he seemed happy enough.

The day after Helen told us that Richard had asked her to marry him, Julie and Christopher came round with some news of their own. She was pregnant again.

Later, as we lay in bed, Mick and me talked about what was happening, Helen was settled again and Julie was hopefully going to make us grandparents again. After we'd talked for a few minutes, we lay side by side thinking our own thoughts. I knew what mine were and when Mick said, 'She'll be starting school soon, won't she,' I didn't need to ask who he was talking about. We'd been thinking similar things.

'I think so,' I said. Mary would have been about four and a half then.

## SUSAN

When I dressed Mary in her school uniform on her first day at school it took everything I had not to take it off her again and keep her at home with me. How could she be old enough for school? She wasn't even five yet. In my heart, though, I knew she was ready. She was growing up fast.

Mary was a chatty kid and never more so that on that day. She had so many questions. Would she like school? Would she like her teacher? What would she learn? She asked all these and a hundred others. She'd woken up way before normal and had wanted to get dressed in her uniform almost as soon as she was up. She was so excited and, despite everything, so was I.

She was still chatting away as I washed her face and helped her to brush her teeth, and she was still at it as she wriggled into the uniform that I had taken such care to iron the night before. Then, there was just time for the finishing touches. I gently pulled the brush through her long, blonde hair over and over until it was as smooth as silk and was so glossy that it almost shone. I got quite emotional doing it, even though I'd brushed her hair thousands of times before.

How different her hair was to mine at her age. I was on auto-pilot as I brushed and my mind started to wander until a four-year-old saying, 'Plait, Mummy, plait,' brought me back to the here and now. I looked at her in the mirror and saw that she was looking at me.

I loved the times that I brushed Mary's hair, it was so intimate and I always felt so close to her. In response to her impatience I separated her hair into three strands and set about forming the hairstyle that my daughter preferred. I'd bought some satin ribbon in the same shade of green as her school cardigan and I secured the plait in place with an elastic band before covering it with the ribbon tied in a bow. She looked perfect.

She was ready for her first day at school.

I had a lot of time to think that day. It was the first time since the day that I'd left home that I'd had the whole day just to myself and I wasn't sure what to do. I set about making a chocolate cake when I got home from the school and as that was baking I cleaned the living room and made the beds. I thought about scrubbing the kitchen floor and maybe the bathroom too but if I did those now, what would I have to occupy myself with the next day? So, after the cake was cooled and iced and the living room was sparkling, I had nothing else to do but sit in a chair and watch the clock hands move round until it was time to collect Mary.

Back then there wasn't a lot in the way of daytime television so I picked up my book and tried to read but I couldn't concentrate and after a while I stopped trying. In the end there was nothing else to do but give in to the thoughts that my mind was trying to have.

My mind went to where it had wanted to go that morning when I was brushing Mary's hair, back to my first day at school. Had my mum felt the way I had? Somehow I had my doubts, but who knew? Had she felt the sense of loss that I was feeling now? My daughter's baby days were behind her and, while I was excited that she was starting a new adventure, I couldn't help grieving for the babyhood that she was leaving behind.

Look, I know I'm not making any sense, but anyone who has had a child that they have had to send off to school will know how I am feeling. I hadn't been the only one at the school gates that morning with a tear in their eye. Had mum had a tear in her eye on my first day at school?

Had Mum ever had a tear in her eye for me?

I was, and am, immensely proud of my daughter. It wasn't an easy life and I won't pretend it was. We didn't have a lot of money for treats, or even the necessities sometimes, but we managed and we did it together, just the two of us. But that morning I'd noticed that not many of the new starters were there with just one parent: most had two and some even had grandparents as well. The first day of school was a family occasion but I was all the family Mary had ever known. Her only other real points of reference were Mandy and Jade who were a family just like us. I don't think she knew at that point what an aunt or an uncle was – they weren't words she had ever had to use – but how long would it be before children that she met at school mentioned aunts, uncles and all the rest? She'd already asked a couple of questions about daddies when the kids at nursery had made Father's Day cards. She wanted to know who she was supposed to give her card to. Where was her daddy? Did she even have one? I've always tried to be honest with Mary and told her that yes she did have a daddy but he was a long way away and we couldn't send him the card right then. Children have a way of taking in the information they want and dismissing the rest so I was relieved when she said that she would keep the card until she could send it to him. She probably did keep the card, for a while at least, but I doubt she still has it now.

I silently thanked God when the clock had moved around to quarter to three and it was time to go and fetch Mary. The thinking was on hold, at least for a while.

Mandy gave me a hug when we met at the school gates. 'It'll get easier,' she told me and asked me what I had done to fill the time. I told her about the cake and the cleaning but left out the bit about the hours sitting in the chair thinking and reminiscing.

Suddenly the schoolyard was full of children and I looked for Mary. There were children everywhere but I saw her when she was still halfway across the yard. She ran the last few yards and I opened my arms up and caught her when she jumped.

As soon as Jade appeared a couple of minutes later, the four of us walked away from the school together. I watched Mary and Jade holding hands skipping along just a couple of feet in front of Mandy and me and in my mind I was ten years old going home from school with Maggie. We had skipped home from school and we had been happy. Mary looked happy.

Once we had left Mandy and Jade at their front gate, Mary and I walked the rest of the way home holding hands together and Mary couldn't help having the occasional skip. She was so happy, and I was happy for her, not to mention a little relieved that her first day seemed to have gone so well. I asked her to tell me about her day and it was like a tap being opened. She told me about Mrs Riley, her teacher, and the story that she had read to them that afternoon. She told me about Molly, the girl that she sat next to in class, and then she told me anything else she could remember. It came in no particular order, just as it popped into her mind.

She was still talking about her day as we sat together at the kitchen table eating the cake that I had made. She talked all of the time and got excited when she remembered something new. She only stopped when she went to bed because she was asleep as soon as her head hit the pillow.

That night, as I sat in the living room of the home that I'd made for us I couldn't help but start thinking again. I told myself that there was no point dwelling on things but I couldn't help myself. It was as if Mum and the past were all that my mind wanted to turn to. I reminded myself yet again of what my mum would say and that was that I had made my bed so I would have to lie in it. That saying only strikes me as funny now, right at this moment as I'm talking to you, because Mum would always remake my bed again after I had done it. Don't know why I've never thought of that before … the mind is a funny thing.

217

Anyway, to get back to the bed that I had made, I didn't mind lying in it, most of the time anyway. I've said before that I did get lonely sometimes, especially at that part of the day when Mary was in bed and I only had myself for company. I didn't mind most of the time but, now and again, it would have been nice to have someone to share my life or even just an evening with.

Mandy said that I needed a boyfriend.

Mandy had another boyfriend by that point. There'd been a few so I can't remember which one exactly. Sometimes, if she was going to be out overnight, Jade would stay with us, otherwise Mandy's neighbour would babysit. I'd only had the one date since Mary had been born, since Tim really, and well remembered how that had ended. I wasn't in a rush to put myself through that again. Was this what my life was going to be like for ever?

The television did not make good company so I went to bed early. That night, before I went to sleep, I decided I should give Julie a ring again, though I didn't really know what I was going to say.

The next morning Mary was already awake when I went into her bedroom. She was sitting up in bed, chatting away to her teddy, telling him that she had to go out today but she'd be back later to tell him about her day. She was so adorable.

I did ring Julie that day but there was no answer. Instead there was a machine saying that they weren't there but if I'd like to leave a name and number they would get back to me.

Answer machines were pretty new back then and I hadn't spoke to one much so I was a bit thrown. Not that I've ever got used to them and I still hate talking to them now. But anyway, I said who it was and that I hoped everyone was all right and that Mary had started school the day before and that she liked it. I also told Julie that I was sorry that I hadn't been in touch for a while but I'd call again soon.

Maybe I would.

Mary soon settled into the way of going to school and I developed a new routine of my own. I cleaned the house every day but to be honest it didn't need it most days and I sometimes used to find myself polishing things that already sparkled. Mum would have been proud of the way I kept the house. I had developed her habits of having a day for every job without even realising it. It was a good way of working.

Mary had been at school for about six months when I met Miriam in the High Street. Do you remember Miriam? She was Mandy's next door neighbour when we lived in Palmer's Court. Well, she was just coming out of the butcher's when I was on my way to the Post Office.

'Well, I'll be blowed,' she said. 'If it isn't Susan Thompson.'

I hadn't seen her at first, her face was hidden under a big red head scarf, but I recognised her voice as soon as I heard it. 'Miriam,' I said, 'how are you?' I hadn't seen her since we'd moved houses.

'Not so bad, love, not so bad,' she said, but I wasn't sure I believed her. 'Just the usual, you know, bloody arthritis.'

It was so good to see her. I thought about her and the other people that had lived in the flats a lot. Once upon a time they had been like family to me. Yet another family that I had lost touch with. Miriam asked me if I'd like to go for a cuppa and a catch up and I jumped at the chance.

We went to a café over the road from the Post Office where she must have been a regular because she shouted her order to the girl behind the counter who called Miriam by name. Miriam had asked for her 'usual for two' and the girl said she would bring it over.

It was lovely to see her but I couldn't help noticing how she had aged in the couple of years since I had seen her last. How old was Miriam? I had no idea but I couldn't think of anyone I'd ever seen who looked older.

She asked how Mary was and said she didn't believe it when I told her that she had started school. She asked how I liked where I was living now and I said it was fine. I told her that Mary liked having her own room and a little garden to play in. She asked me how Mandy and Jade were and I told her that Jade was in the class above Mary and that Mandy had a new boyfriend. All just general chit chat, until Miriam said:

'And what about your mum?'

'What about her?'

'Have you still not spoken to her?'

She made it sound like a bad thing and truth be told, I knew that it was, I hadn't spoken to my mother in over five years.

'No. I've spoken to my sister a couple of times though. In fact, I rang her the other day.'

'How are things at home?'

'I don't know,' I admitted, 'she wasn't in. I just left a message on her answer machine.'

We sat in silence for a few moments as the waitress brought over our drinks. There was a piece of Bakewell tart for each of us too.

'Can't have tea without a bit of cake,' Miriam said as she spooned sugar into her drink and stirred it slowly. 'It's a treat for me now 'cause of my diabetes, but when my littl'uns were growing up there was always a cake in the tin.'

Littl'uns? What did she mean?

'Surprises you, does it,' she said, looking up from her cup, 'that I have children?'

'I've never heard you talk about them before. I just assumed that you didn't have any,' I said.

'Might as well not have for all I see of them.' She didn't try to hide the sadness from her voice.

I didn't know what to say so I waited for her to speak again.

'I have a son, Thomas.'

I couldn't help but see the tears that were forming as she added:

'He lives in New Zealand. He was in the navy and met a lass from over there and married her. They've got a couple of kids but I've never seen them. And then I have a daughter, Brenda, and God knows where she is.'

Silence.

'We had a falling out, you see, about her choice of boyfriend. She was all for this lad who was into drinking – and drugs as well, probably – and said that she was going to marry him. I said over my dead body she would and the next thing I knew she'd run off with him.'

I could only sit and watch her as she looked at me.

'But do you know what, Susan? There's not a day goes by that I don't think of them, especially Brenda. At least I know that Thomas is settled, well I think he is, but I don't know anything about Brenda. I don't know where she is or how she is.' She reached across the table and took hold of my hand, 'And your mum will be the same love.' I shook my head and Miriam shook my hand. 'Yes she will, Susan. Trust me, I know.'

'My mum wanted to hide me away in the country until my baby was born so that I could give the baby away and no one would ever know about it, about her, about Mary.'

'Mary didn't exist to your mum,' Miriam said. 'Only you existed; you, her daughter. Now I don't know your mother but I think we've all got something in common and that's that at the end of the day we want what's best for our children. We want them to be better than we were.' She squeezed my hand again, 'Your mother just had a funny way of showing it.'

I shook my head. 'No, she's not like that.'

Something happened to me that day and I finally opened up to someone. 'She never wanted me you know,' I told her. 'I walked in on my sisters talking one day and they said that mum had never wanted me. She didn't pay me any attention when I was growing up; I was always in the way. She never

223

sat me down and combed my hair until it shone and then tied it up with pretty ribbons. She ignored me most of the time; I was just in the way. And then when I got pregnant, she told me that I'd brought shame on the family, that's why she wanted me to give my baby away. My baby, my Mary, was a dirty little secret that needed to be hidden from the neighbours.'

Two more cups of tea arrived without me even realising that Miriam had ordered them. She started to add sugar to her fresh cup. 'Like I've told you before, love,' she said, 'for your mum, Mary did not exist as a person. If she met her now, she would see what a sweetheart she is and she would love her.'

'I can't go back now. How would she explain it to the neighbours? According to Julie she's told them that I enjoyed Scarborough so much that I decided to stay there.'

'Yes, well, if she came up with something to explain your disappearance I'm sure she'd find another reason for your return.'

'And Mary's?'

'Look, it's your decision, but if you want a bit of advice from a very old woman give your mum a second chance … before it's too late.'

I said I'd think about it. And I did think about it; I thought about it long and hard and, after I had, I was torn. Like I've said a million times, I loved my mother and all I ever wanted was to be loved in return but could I risk being rejected again? And, more than that, could I risk Mary being rejected? Did my mother think about me every day as Miriam said she did her own children? Miriam said that all mothers had something in common so, being one myself, I tried to put myself in my mother's position. How would I react? Was Miriam right about Mum only wanting to do what was best for me? I've said before that I believed making the problem disappear was probably the only way out she could see. One thing was certain, though. I knew for a fact that, if I was in her situation and regardless of what had happened between us, I would always love Mary and want to know how she was.

I don't think I slept a wink that night, I just lay awake thinking about what Miriam had said and the things that had occurred to me since that conversation. A lot of things made sense now, especially the way that Miriam had treated both Mandy and me. We'd just thought it was because she was a nice old lady who was kind to us, but now I realised she was compensating for the family of her own that she couldn't see. Somehow I couldn't see my mum behaving the same

225

way to make up for Mary and me not being there, but who knew? What if she *was* missing me? That thought had never occurred to me. What if she was sorry that things had turned out the way they had? Would that make any difference? I needed to give it a lot more thought.

Three days later my world was blown apart.

I was standing at the school gates waiting for Mary to come out of school when Mandy appeared beside me. She was red-faced and out of breath as though she had been running.

'You're not going to believe it,' she said in between breaths.

'What's wrong?' I had no idea what was going on and I couldn't help being worried. Mandy was usually calm and cocky.

'I saw Dan and Louise in town,' she said when she had got her breath back, 'you know the ones that live next door to Bob at Palmer's Court. You'll never guess what they told me.'

'That's funny,' I said, 'I saw Miriam the other day. We haven't seen any of them in years and then both of us in the same week.'

She had a funny look on her face. 'You never said you saw Miriam. How was she?'

226

'She seemed fine, said her arthritis was playing her up.'

'Yes, well, Bob found her dead on the kitchen floor this morning.'

'What?'

Mandy explained that Bob had been walking along the landing and happened to glance through the kitchen window of Miriam's flat and saw her lying face down on the floor in her dressing gown. He rang for an ambulance but by the time the police broke the door down she was dead. Louise said that the paramedic reckoned she'd been there all night.

I don't know if I went white but I knew that I felt sick. 'I don't believe it,' I said and I had to struggle to control my breathing. I didn't want to break down at the school gates.

'I know. Poor old Miriam.' She stroked my arm.

'I just saw her the other day,' I said, again. 'We were talking just the other day. She said th–'

I stopped mid-sentence when I remembered what she had said. I blew out my cheeks and looked straight into Mandy's eyes. 'She said that' – I could hear my voice shaking – 'she thought I should contact my mum…' I paused before the last bit, '…before it's too late.'

I told Mandy about Miriam's children, about the son that she hadn't seen for years and the daughter who could be anywhere. I told her how Miriam reckoned that my mother would be thinking about me every day, wondering where I was and how I was doing.

'Bloody hell,' Mandy said as the sound of children running got louder.

When I caught sight of Mary running towards me I forced a smile onto my face.

The following week Mandy and I went to Miriam's funeral. We'd gone to the library to read what Mum used to call the hatched matched and dispatched report in the local paper and read her obituary there. Mum always said that you could tell a lot by what was written in the paper after you died. Miriam's didn't say much at all. It gave her name, that she was a mother and grandmother and the details of her funeral. No 'much loved' this or 'beloved' that; just the bare details.

On the morning of the funeral, Mary had asked me why I was wearing the clothes that I was. I was wearing a black skirt with a white blouse under a black cardigan. Mary had probably never seen me in a skirt before. I told her that I was going to say goodbye to a friend of mine who was going away and I thanked God when she didn't ask me where my friend was going.

The funeral was at 10 o'clock on a Friday morning and Mandy and I went straight to the crematorium after we'd

228

dropped the girls off at school. I'd never been to a funeral before so I didn't know quite what to expect, but I had thought there'd be more of a turnout. There were just her neighbours from Palmer's Court and three old ladies who turned out to be the friends that she used to go to bingo with on a Tuesday afternoon.

Louise and Dan stood with Bob at one side of the open double door and the ladies at the other. We smiled at the ladies but went to stand with our former neighbours.

Louise gave us both a hug. 'I'm glad you've both come,' she said, 'Miriam would have liked you to come.'

'Aye,' Dan chipped in. 'Haven't seen you in ages and then Lou happens to bump into Mandy and tell her about the old lass. They say God works in mysterious ways.'

'I saw her just the other week,' I told them. 'She seemed fine – well as fine as she ever did.'

'She said that she'd seen you and that you'd gone for a cup of tea together and had a catch up.' Louise looked at me and then Mandy. 'Miriam was very fond of you girls you know.'

'And we were fond of her.' I knew that I could speak for both of us.

Just then there was the sound of tyres on gravel as the hearse pulled up. I looked for another car, the one with her family in it, but it wasn't there. There was just the hearse. Miriam's family was nowhere in sight and huge, hot, wet tears formed in my eyes. How could they not be here? Louise put her arm round my shoulder and squeezed it.

As we followed the coffin into the crematorium, 'Amazing Grace' came out of the speakers on the wall. I'd once heard Miriam singing it to Mary when she was a baby and the memory brought more tears to my eyes. They just fell down my cheeks and off the end of my chin until Louise handed me a tissue and I wiped them away.

Miriam's coffin was placed on a stand inside an alcove at the front of the building. A man in a suit seemed to be directing proceedings and when the pall bearers had disappeared back down the aisle he turned to us and welcomed us to what he called a celebration of our 'dear friend's life.' To be honest, it wasn't much of a celebration because he'd said all he had to say in less than five minutes, the curtains had closed in front of Miriam's coffin and a song about eternal love was coming out of the speakers. Louise did tell me who it was singing but I'd never heard of them – never heard the song before either.

The ladies from the bingo nodded their goodbyes to us and walked away. The rest of us stood around like none of us knew what to do next.

'We should do something to remember her by,' Dan said, 'give her a bit of a send-off.'

In the end we decided to go to the café that she and I had visited just a couple of weeks earlier. Miriam wasn't a drinker but she did like her tea and Louise said that she'd visited that café at least twice a week for years. It seemed appropriate.

'Miriam's usual for five,' I said to the girl behind the counter and no one disagreed. We sat at the same table that Miriam and I had and I couldn't help but wonder if that had been her usual table. I decided to believe that it was.

The tea's came along with a portion of Bakewell tart for each of us and we all tucked into Miriam's usual. We chatted about how we all were. They asked how we liked it over on the estate, how the girls were doing, that sort of thing. We asked how they liked their new neighbours and were they all keeping well. After another round of Miriam's special it was time to say our goodbyes.

Dan and Bob were already out the door with Mandy close behind them when Louise grabbed at my arm to hold me back.

'You all right?' I asked.

She looked through the door to where the other three stood on the pavement talking before she turned back to me and took a deep breath. 'Miriam said that I was to tell you something if I ever saw you again,' she said.

'Oh?' I was very curious.

'Just a couple of days before she died she came into my kitchen when I was making the tea and told me that if I ever saw you again I was to tell you to think on what she had said.' I wasn't looking at her but I could feel her eyes on me. 'She didn't say any more than that so do you know what she was talking about?'

Oh yes, I knew what she was talking about.

After we left the café, Louise, Dan and Bob went one way and Mandy and I went the other. We all promised not to let it be so long next time.

'What was all that about with Louise?' Mandy asked

'All what about?' I said, trying to act dumb, but Mandy just raised an eyebrow at me as if to say *you know fine what I'm talking about.*

She knew me so well. 'Miriam talked to Louise a couple of days before she died,' I said, 'and told her, if she ever saw me again, to tell me I had to think on what we had spoken about.'

'But Miriam knew your story, didn't she? She knew about your mum wanting to send you away and have Mary adopted.'

'Yes, she knew all of that.' We'd reached the bus stop by then; there were just the two of us there. 'But like I've told you, she said that there wouldn't be a day goes past that my mum wouldn't think about me, wouldn't wonder where I was, or how I was. She said that she thought of her son and daughter every day. She asked me how I would feel if it was Mary that had run away.'

Mandy isn't often lost for words and I think that was the first time that I saw it happen, so I took advantage of it and carried on talking.

'The thing is Mandy that I know if it was Mary I would never stop thinking about her, not for one second of one day. I would always wonder where she was, if she was safe, what she was doing. I don't think that I could live without knowing all of those things.'

'But that's you and Mary.'

'I'm still her daughter Mandy, and if Miriam was right, she really was only trying to do what was best for me, or rather, what *she* thought was best for me.'

'Well she had a funny way of going about it.'

'She was a very funny woman.'

We both laughed.

'But do you know what, Mandy?' It was time to admit the truth. 'There's hardly a day goes by that I don't think about her too.'

***

I did think on what Miriam had said. I thought about nothing else all afternoon. I also thought about Miriam's children. Did they even know that their mother was dead? Surely someone had contacted her son? Maybe not, because surely if they had he would have come to his own mother's funeral, no matter what had happened between them over the years. New Zealand wasn't the moon; there were planes. Louise had said that Miriam had organised and paid for her own funeral, it was as though she was resigned to the fact that there would be no family to take care of such things. But how could there be if they didn't know she was dead? I was going round in circles around myself and the only thing that I knew for sure was that I could be that daughter, the one that wasn't at their own mother's funeral because I didn't know they were dead. I didn't think I wanted to be that person.

The deal was clinched that afternoon when I picked Mary up from school. She came running across the yard clutching a parcel wrapped up in pink tissue paper.

'What's that?' I asked her.

'A present for you,' she said.

For me? Why? Of course. It would be Mother's Day in two days' time.

She held on to it all the way home and then put it on a shelf and told me that I couldn't have it until Sunday. She looked at it every now and then as though making sure it was still there.

'Have you got a present for your mummy?' She asked later on, when we were sitting at the table eating our tea. She just came out with it, there was no warning and her question took me by surprise. What was I supposed to say to her?

I settled for: 'No.'

She looked at me across the table with her knife and fork held upright in her tiny hands. 'Why?' And then, as she went back to attacking her spaghetti hoops on toast she asked, 'Where is your mummy?'

She'd never asked about my parents before but I guess school was opening her up to lots of things, like family for instance. Oh, sod it. I took a deep breath.

'My mummy lives in a different town and I haven't seen her for a long time. Not since before you were born.'

She didn't look up from her task of getting as many hoops on the fork as she could. 'Why?'

Oh well, in for a penny and all that. 'We fell out.'

Now she looked up. 'You fell out?'

235

'Yes.'

'With your mummy?' It was as though it was beyond her comprehension, which to be fair, it probably was. She stared at me with those big eyes of hers and for the first time I realised that they were my mother's eyes. How had I never seen that before? Maybe I had just not wanted to acknowledge it. 'You won't ever fall out with me will you?'

I pushed myself away from the table and so did she. I fell to my knees on the carpet and let her run into my arms. 'No, my darling,' I said to her. 'I will never fall out with you.' I hugged her and felt I never wanted to let her go.

That night when she was safely tucked up in bed I got the bus timetable out of my bag and scoured it. There was one bus to my home town on Sunday and it left at eleven o'clock. I would be there on Mother's Day. I was going home.

## JEAN

I thought about Susan a lot, and not just Susan; I thought about her daughter Mary too. Sometimes I wondered how I could possibly have a granddaughter that I had never seen. I wondered who she looked like. That Tim Preston had had a baby with another lass a couple of years earlier and when I saw her baby there was no denying it was his. Is that what my granddaughter looked like? I hoped not because I still couldn't stand the sight of Tim Preston and if I did ever see him I would walk in the opposite direction. He'd stopped me once and asked after Susan. I'd said that she was all the better for having him out of her life.

But she hadn't just got him out of her life, had she? We'd gone from her life too.

I tried to tell myself that no news was good news and that if anything was wrong we would have heard. Surely she would have had something on her that would have directed the police to us if anything was really wrong. It helped to think that.

Julie got a phone call from her in the September that Mary would have been about five. 'What did she say? Is she all right?' Me and her dad couldn't get the questions out quick enough; it had been so long since she'd called. But Julie couldn't answer our questions because she'd been at the doctor's. Susan had left a message saying that they were all right, that Mary had started school and that she liked it.

'Was that it?' I don't think I hid my disappointment.

Apparently Susan had said that she would call again soon and I hoped that she would. Mick told Julie that if Susan rang again to ask her to ring us too. I hoped that she would because it had been such a long time since I'd heard her voice, and even though I could still hear it in my head I wanted to hear it with my ears. I missed her more than I could ever have imagined I would so I couldn't begin to imagine how Mick felt. To me she was my daughter but he hadn't seen or spoken to his princess in over five years, and it was starting to show on him.

I knew he wasn't getting any younger but he looked older than his years and I knew that was down to Susan going away. He missed her so much. And so did I.

I'd been so angry with her at the beginning, for getting pregnant in the first place and then for running away when all I was I trying to do was what I thought was best for her. But she hadn't seen it that way and over the years I'd started to question if I had been right. Had there been another option? Could she have kept her baby and stayed at home? Could she have been another of the unmarried mothers that were popping up all over the place? I wouldn't have liked it, of that I was certain, but maybe I could have got used to it. Could she have got used to the comments and the looks? What was the point in asking questions that I would never know the answers to?

I imagined that she was still on her own. I'd told her she'd struggle to find a man to take on another man's child. I know it did happen now and then, but not often and I hadn't wanted Susan to risk her happiness on being one of the lucky ones. Luck wasn't big in our family.

I would sit some nights and wonder what sort of mother I was. I'd tried my best. I'd kept a clean house and my girls were always well turned out but somehow I'd ended up with one daughter who was divorced and another who had run away from home. Not the perfect family that you saw on the television.

***

Celebration times were the worst – you know, Christmas, birthdays that sort of thing. I didn't even know when my granddaughter's birthday was. I thought it was some time in October but I didn't know for sure. The year before I'd bought a card with 'Granddaughter' written on it and kept it in the bedside table. I'd written, 'With love from Gran and Granddad,' on the inside and I looked at it every day. I know its silly but I was getting sentimental in my old age.

At least the other two seemed all right and I didn't have to worry too much about them. I was concerned for Julie because she was terrified that she would lose this baby as well but once she got past the point that she lost the first one she calmed down a bit, and the doctors all told her that everything seemed fine this time. Helen was busy with wedding plans of course. She and Richard wanted to be married quickly and at first I thought that she might be pregnant too but it turned out that they were just in love and wanted to be together. We saw a lot more of her now that she wasn't worried about what Robert's mother might think and I was glad of that. I liked Richard, he was good to Helen and to James and that was all I could ask. His family were nice too; more our kind of people.

They were going to get married at the register office, which wasn't my idea of a wedding at all but what could you do when they had both been married and divorced. At least it would be legal. There would be no white dress and fancy reception this time, just the register office and then a meal in a local restaurant. Hopefully this one would last.

So Helen was getting a second chance with marriage and Julie was getting a second chance at being a mum. I hoped and prayed that I would get a second chance with Susan.

Like I said before, celebrations were the worst, and worst of all by far was Mother's Day. It was just around the corner and Julie had suggested that we go out for dinner. I didn't want to sound ungrateful but I didn't fancy it. I wasn't one for shows like that and to be honest I'd never had a Sunday dinner out that was a patch on mine. I offered to cook for them instead and they agreed it might be for the best. Helen wouldn't be able to make it for lunch but she said that they would be round later. Richard would be away in Swansea that weekend visiting his grandma and Helen and James were going with him.

At least my nest would be partly full and I would have to make do with that.

## MICK

Appearances were everything to Jean – always have been, always will be – it's just the way she is. It's not her fault really; it's how she was brought up – how we were all brought up, it's just that Jean didn't move with the times.

I mean, when she fell wrong with Helen there was never any doubt that I would marry her. I knew that I had to face up to my responsibilities and I also knew that, if I hadn't, her brothers would have found me and rearranged my face. I'm not sure that we'd have got married if she hadn't been pregnant but she was and we did and to be honest, things could have been a lot worse.

She has always kept a clean house, always fed me well and looked after the money and she gave me three beautiful daughters, which is a miracle because if she'd had the choice I think we'd have stopped after one. Helen was an accident, Julie was a surprise and I think she looked at Susan as a bit of a disaster. She was a good wife who didn't deny me but she was never very keen on the physical side of our marriage. She did what she thought was her duty and the girls were an unwanted bi-product of that.

242

But that was us, in our day. If you got pregnant, or you got a girl pregnant, you got married, simple as that. I knew what was expected, she knew what was expected, so we did it and once we had done it we were married for life. We didn't expect marriage to be easy, nobody did; it was something that had to be worked at and you took the bad with the good.

But things could have been different for Susan.

I know that there would have been some talk from the neighbours but we could have got through that. Yes, they'd have been talking about her but that's what they do and they'd have got over it and gone on to something else soon enough. Jean didn't see it that way though. In her mind there was no way that Susan could have kept her baby I should have seen that. I'd agreed to ring my cousin to ask if Susan could go and stay with her but I'd told Jean to tell her that she wouldn't have to give her baby away. I shouldn't have done that; I should have told Susan myself.

I should have known that Susan would find a way of keeping her baby because I knew she would be more interested in facing up to her responsibilities and doing the right thing than in what the neighbours thought – she was like me in that respect. Jean had seemed surprised when Susan ran away but I wasn't. I hadn't expected it but once she had done it I realised that there was nothing else she could have done. She knew that if she'd stayed, her mum would have found a way of getting her own way. Jean was like that. No matter what any of us wanted, Jean always managed to get her own way. Susan wasn't going to let that happen this time so she had done the only thing she could and I was proud of her – though I had to keep that to myself.

I saw her that night, the one she ran away. She was sitting in a café at the bus station. She was right at the back and she looked straight at me. I think she probably expected me to walk in there and drag her home, but I didn't. Her mum would have but that's the reason I made sure it was me that went out looking for her. I didn't know what Susan's plan was but I trusted that she was doing the right thing and I had to give her the chance to get on with it.

I almost went inside to talk to her but I knew that if I had I might not have been able to let her go. For her to save her baby, I had to let mine go. I blew her a kiss and walked quickly away and as I did my heart was breaking. I had to walk around for ages before I went home just to make sure that the tears had stopped.

I didn't tell Jean that I'd seen her. Well, I did later on but not right then, not that night. No, I saved that until one night when we were having a row about Susan and what had happened. I hadn't meant to say it but it was out before I knew it and once it was said there was no taking it back. I was hurting and I blamed Jean for that. I wanted to hurt her too. If I'd brought Susan back that night Jean would have found a way of controlling the situation, like she always did. I wanted her to know that I had stopped that from happening. I've never really stood up to Jean, there's never been much point, but I wanted her to know that, when it really mattered, I had.

We found a way of living together, we had to, and it wasn't always easy. It was just the two of us at home so we didn't have to make the effort to pretend that everything was all right. Things got better after that first phone call from Susan. She'd phoned Julie to say that she'd had the baby, a daughter that she'd called Mary though none of us knew where that name had come from. Susan had said that they were both all right but she didn't say where they were.

After that phone call, I relaxed a bit. Before that, I'd just had to hope that she'd known what she was doing and that she was safe. I still didn't know where she was and we only had her word that they were all right but I believed what she'd told Julie because Jean might have thought she knew Susan, but I knew her better and I knew that if there was a real problem, if that baby of hers was in any danger, she would have asked for help. She'd risked everything to have that baby, after all.

So with my mind at rest I was able to be more of what a husband should be to Jean. I'm not saying that things were back to what they had been but they were better. As times passed I could see that she was missing Susan too, not that she ever admitted it. She never said that she thought she'd handled things badly but I could see that she was having second thoughts.

We didn't hear from Susan again for a long time. At first, every time I saw Julie I asked if Susan had called her but the answer was always the same: no, she hadn't. I stopped after a while because I didn't want to put Julie in an awkward situation. Maybe Susan was ringing her but asking her to say nothing to us. I trusted Julie to tell us if there was anything that we needed to know.

Anyway, Julie had problems of her own. She'd been having a baby but lost it and the poor kid was in bits. My heart went out to her. Everyone, especially her mother, said that it was just one of those things and that there'd be other babies but that didn't help. I kept my mouth shut. What did I know about that sort of thing? I just held her when she cried.

So we had that with Julie and then Helen and her husband split up. He was carrying on with another woman and for two pins I'd have gone and knocked his head off but Helen and her mother wouldn't hear of it. Helen said that wasn't the way things were done these days and I think Jean just didn't want me arrested for assault. Wouldn't have bothered me. I never liked the lad much anyway.

Things have turned out better for Julie and Chris though. They told us not long ago that they are having another baby and we've all got fingers crossed that everything will be all right this time. The doctors are keeping a close eye on her and she hasn't got long to go now.

She was at the doctor's when the second phone call from Susan came. Thank God they had one of those answer machines because at least Susan was able to leave a message. She'd said that Mary had started school and that she liked it. It wasn't a lot to go on but it would have to do, for now.

I say 'for now' because, through everything, I knew that Susan would come home one day. We just had to wait until she was ready.

I've missed Susan something terrible in the years that she's been gone and every night before I go to sleep I pray to God that Susan will come home tomorrow.

My prayers were answered. Susan turned up today.

## SUSAN

I could feel the eyes of the curtain twitchers on us as Mary and I walked down the street towards the house that I'd left nearly six years earlier. Nothing had changed; it looked just the same as it always had. Tommy Brown's car was still sitting on bricks in their front garden and Old Mrs Murton still dried her washing in hers. On the surface it was like I had never been away but the reality was that I was a different person now. My heart was beating against my rib cage and I squeezed Mary's tiny hand hoping to get some strength from it.

I was terrified. What would be waiting for me when I knocked on the door? Would anything be waiting for me? Maybe they were out. Who was I kidding? It was Sunday and it was lunchtime; of course they would be in. But what would be waiting for me? Well I'd find out soon enough.

'Where are we, Mummy?' Mary asked.

'This is your grandparents' house,' I told her as I lifted the latch on the gate. 'This is where my mummy and daddy live,' or at least I hoped that they still did. It had never occurred to me that they might have moved. Half a dozen steps later we were standing in front of the door and I watched my hand shake as I made a fist and knocked.

I waited for what felt like ages with my stomach doing somersaults and a sick feeling burning my throat but no one came. I lifted my hand to knock again and as I did I heard the sound of voices – well one voice – on the other side of the door. I'd heard Julie shout that she would get the door and I thanked God that she was there.

The door opened and for the first time in six years I was looking at a family member that wasn't my daughter.

Julie's mouth opened wide and moved but no words came out. She grabbed hold of the door jamb like she needed to hold herself up. I noticed the large bump on her stomach and I felt a little bolt of happiness shoot through me. Julie was having a baby.

I felt Mary tighten her grip on my hand. God only knows what she was thinking.

'Hello, Julie,' I said. 'Are you all right?'

Still her mouth was moving and still no words came out. I heard another voice from behind her ask if she was all right and a moment later I was looking at my mother. She looked older, which I know sounds stupid because obviously she was older, we all were, but she looked *old*.

'You'd better come inside,' Mum said. I looked down at Mary who was looking up at me with wide eyes.

'Come on, sweetheart,' I said as calmly as I could. I gave her hand a gentle squeeze. We walked through the door together and as we passed Mum in the hallway I noticed that she popped her head out of the door and cast a glance up and down the street.

She leaned into the door to close it and rested her head against it for a few seconds.

When she turned round we stood looking at each other. From somewhere behind me I could hear my dad talking to someone about football while in the hallway my mother and I just stood and looked at each other. Mum was moving her tongue over her lips, trying to moisten them and I knew how she felt because my mouth was as dry as a bone.

'Hello,' the voice came from my left-hand side and I looked down to see my daughter looking up at my mother. 'I'm Mary.'

My mum looked down at her too and after a couple of deep breaths she found her voice. 'Hello, Mary,' she croaked. 'I'm … your gran.'

'Hello, Gran. I'm very pleased to meet you.'

Mum smiled as the two of them looked at each other and her face was softer than I had ever seen it before.

'Why don't we go and meet your Granddad,' Julie said, holding her hand out to Mary who looked at me for guidance. I nodded my head. 'I'm your Auntie Julie by the way,' she said as they disappeared into the living room.

Mum and I still stood looking at each other.

'You look well,' Mum said.

'Thanks. I am well.' On the outside I was calm but inside was a different story. What is it they say about swans? That they look all serene on top of the water but underneath their feet are going like the clappers. Well I knew how they must feel.

'Where have you been?' Mum was also calm though I suspect that was just on the outside too.

I told her and she made a comment about how it was supposed to be nice there. I said something about it having good and bad in it, like all places do, and for a couple of minutes we exchanged words but didn't really say anything at all. It was the most surreal conversation of my life. There'd been a hell of a commotion in the living room when Julie had taken Mary in and I'd fully expected Dad to appear in the hallway but he didn't and so Mum and I just carried on looking at each other and speaking without saying anything.

After a few seconds of silence Mum said, 'She looks like...' and I thought she was going to finish the sentence with the word 'Tim' but thank God she didn't. She said '…a lovely little girl,' and I allowed myself to breathe.

'She is.' I looked towards the door that Mary had gone through and said, 'She is an angel.' I felt a defiance rising inside me and I turned to my mum and told her, 'and she was worth everything.'

Mum couldn't hold my gaze. She knew what I meant. My eyes didn't move an inch. I could see that Mum's chest was heaving and I wondered if she was all right. Should I call for help? I'd only meant to make a point, not give her a heart attack. One of my reasons for coming was so that I could reconnect while I still had time. I didn't want that time to be less than five minutes.

But Mum recovered herself and lifted her head. Her voice was low, not much more than a whisper really. 'I was trying to do what I thought was best for you.'

I considered that for a second or two and then told her, 'and so was I.'

Just then the door to the living room opened and my dad was there. Like Mum, he had aged a lot in the last six years and I knew that I was probably the cause of that. He opened his arms wide and wrapped them around me. We both cried.

After we'd all had a cup of tea, the cure for everything in my mum's house, she said she had to put the finishing touches to the lunch. She asked if we were stopping for it and I said that our bus back home didn't leave until five o'clock so that would be 'lovely, thank you.'

Anyway, while Mum was off in the kitchen doing what she did best, which was the Sunday roast, I sat in the living room and chatted with my dad and Julie and Chris. I'd brought some toys in a bag to keep Mary entertained on the bus journey and she sat on the floor playing with them. Dad was talking to me but he could hardly keep his eyes off her. It was as though he could hardly believe she was there.

There were lots of questions. Where did we live? How had I been? Had I made new friends? Was Mary happy in school? Just one after the other with barely any time to answer one before the next one was asked. I had questions of my own too. How were they? How were Helen and Robert? When was Julie's baby due?

Julie told me that she had a couple more weeks to go but twenty minutes later she was on her way to hospital after her waters broke and soaked the sofa. On her way out the door Julie looked at me and asked me to promise that I would stay. I said that I couldn't but I did promise that I'd come back the following weekend. I wished her good luck and told her that it would be worth it.

Mum went back to the kitchen and I was alone with my dad, apart from Mary and she had her head in a book. As Dad and I sat together holding hands he kept repeating, 'I can't believe it,' over and over again. He must have said it half a dozen times.

I could hardly believe it myself.

'I always knew you'd come back,' he said eventually.

Did he? I hadn't known it; for a long time I thought I would never come back.

'You were right,' I said, my voice cracking.

Dad's hand was over his mouth like he was trying to hold something inside but his eyes gave away the smile that was under his hand.

'I have missed you so much, Susan.'

'Oh, Dad,' I got down on my knees and knelt on the floor in front of him. I rested my head on his thigh and he stroked my hair, 'I've missed you too.'

Only then did Mary look up from her book. She looked at me and smiled. I smiled back. Dad and I sat like that for a while and then, when the time was right, I sat back on the sofa.

'How have you been,' he asked, 'really?'

'We've been all right,' I said, 'mostly.'

He didn't ask what I meant by that but he did say that he thought it couldn't have been easy for me. He was right, it hadn't been, but I glossed over the bad times and told him that I had been very lucky.

'So, Julie's having a baby,' I said trying to move the conversation along and then I added, 'now,' and laughed.

'Yes,' he laughed too. 'Please God, everything will be all right this time.'

This time? What did he mean this time? And that was when I found out that my sister had miscarried a baby five years earlier. 'It happened not long after we heard that Mary had been born,' he said and I wondered if Julie had resented me.

What else had I missed? Well, it turned out that I'd missed Robert's affair, Helen's divorce, Robert having a baby with someone else and Helen organising her second wedding to a man called Richard. So much had happened in the time that I had been away – hardly surprising really; a lot had happened to me too. That's how it went. Life moved on and I had been out of their lives for a long time.

Mum called us to the table and, like the street outside, the kitchen looked just the way it always had. Mum told me to sit in my chair, the one that I had always sat in at tea time, and that was when I really felt at home again. Mary sat beside me in what had been – and probably still was – Julie's seat.

I've told you before that no one makes mashed potatoes like my mum and they had never tasted better than they did that day. Mum and Dad couldn't take their eyes off Mary who didn't appear to notice as she tucked into her food.

After lunch I said that I would give Mum a hand with the washing up and I was amazed when she agreed that I could. The kitchen had always been Mum's domain and she wasn't in the habit of letting people help her. She hadn't used to be anyway but something about her was different now.

'Are you happy?' she asked me as she handed me the first plate she'd washed.

'Yes,' I said.

We worked in silence for a while and as we did I realised that the way I worked in my own kitchen, at my own sink, was the way that my mum worked. I know that might sound daft but different people do simple things like washing dishes differently and I did them like my mum did. I truly was my mother's daughter.

Mum put down the plate that she had been washing and turned to me. 'Can you forgive me?' she asked.

I have to say, that stunned me a bit. I had never heard her say those words to anyone before and I certainly hadn't expected to hear them that day. She grabbed the tea towel I was holding, tossed it aside and took hold of my hands. We stood with our wet hands interlocked looking at each other. I could see tears in her eyes and I was sure that she could see them in mine.

'I was wrong,' she said finally. 'I see that now and I am so sorry, but please believe me when I said that I was trying to do what I thought was best for you.'

'You wanted me to give Mary away, Mam.' I know it sounded like an accusation but I hadn't meant it to. I could hear the crack in my voice.

She thought about that for a few seconds, her eyes on the sink like she was expecting the right words to float out of the water. 'I was just thinking about you, Susan. *You*.' She emphasised the word. 'I was just trying to do what was best for my daughter.'

'And so was I.'

We looked at each other, finally understanding that we were just two women who both wanted what was best for their children. After a minute or so Mum put her hands back in the sink and carried on where she had left off but without the vigour that she had started the job with. It was as though the apology had taken everything out of her.

After the dishes were finished we went back to the living room to find my dad sitting in his chair with a five-year-old fast asleep on his lap. I couldn't help myself, I just started to cry.

'Don't cry, love,' Dad said, patting the seat on the sofa that was closest to him. I sat down and rubbed my tears away with the heel of my hand.

'I am so sorry,' I sniffed, looking first at Dad and then at Mum, 'for what I have put you both through.'

'We've all got a lot to be sorry for,' Dad said but he directed his words towards Mum. She avoided his eyes by looking at my daughter who was starting to stir from her sleep.

'She is beautiful,' Mum said with a softness in her voice that I had never heard before and when I looked at her there was something on her face that I had never seen before either. Was that a look of love? Yes. It was. She had a little smile on her lips and was all doe-eyed.

'Yes she is,' I said.

'She's got your eyes, Jean,' Dad said.

'Do you think?' Mum said, not able to keep a hint of pride out of her voice.

Mary woke up fully just after that and Mum couldn't wait for a cuddle. 'Are you going to come and sit on Gran's knee for a bit?' she asked, and Mary duly obliged.

I was amazed by how easily she had taken to these people that she'd only just met but I put it down to something that humans did; you know, recognising their own. I don't know the science but I'm sure there's an explanation for it because Mary was usually wary of strangers.

Then with her usual, 'say it like it is' attitude Mary asked, 'Are you and Mummy friends again?' Her face was upturned and just an inch or two way from Mum's chin.

Mum looked over Mary's head to me and smiled. I smiled back and I think I nodded my head just ever so slightly. 'Yes, Mary,' she said kissing the top of her granddaughter's head. 'Your Mummy and me are friends again.'

In Mary's head that was that: we were all friends again, end of story. Mum asked her questions about school and her friends and Mary answered the only way she knew how which was with absolute honesty. Molly was her best friend in her class but Jade was her best friend in the world. 'Oh,' she said, 'and Jade's mummy is my mummy's best friend.'

'I met her just after I left,' I told them. 'We've been through a lot together.'

They didn't ask where I had gone to and I didn't tell them. What would be the point? What mattered now was that I had come back, and I had brought my daughter with me. The time just flew and before I knew it, it was time to leave. We were going to have to rush to make it to the bus station on time.

As we were preparing to leave something happened that I had wanted all of my life. My mum hugged me. It took me by surprise, but not as much as when she whispered, 'I love you, Susan,' in my ear.

I hugged her back. 'I love you too, Mum.'

We were both crying – in fact, we were all crying apart from Mary. She had a big smile on her face.

I didn't have time to think about anything on our way to the bus station, apart from worrying that we'd miss the bus, but when we were safely sitting down and on our way I had time to reflect on the day. I had been shocked by the change in my parents, especially my mother. My dad had just aged, other than that he'd seemed just the same as he'd always been. But Mum? Well, Mum seemed like a completely different person. She'd asked me if I could forgive her – which is something I had never expected – but, more than that, she had said that she *loved* me. I'd waited all of my life to hear those words.

As the bus moved along I looked out of the window and watched the world go by. I was glad that we had visited and I was thrilled that the day had gone so well, but now I needed to go home and process everything.

When I'd watched Mum doing the dishes I'd seen that I had something in common with her, but now I knew that there were other things too; things far more important than washing dishes. I believed that she was telling the truth when she said that she'd been trying to do what was best for me. I would never accept her idea of what that was but I couldn't argue with the principle. What was best for my child would always be my prime concern too.

Keeping up appearances had meant so much to Mum when I was growing up and I'd really believed that had been the reason she wanted me to go into hiding and then give my baby away without anyone knowing. But maybe I'd been wrong. She'd wanted a different life for me, one that involved a job and a husband before the baby came along. But it was like Miriam had said – like Mum herself had said: to her, Mary hadn't existed. Mum had been thinking only about me. In her world, which I have to say is not always the same world that the rest of us live in, secret adoption was the only way out.

I hadn't understood my mother at all before that day. I'd seen her be the way that she was with the neighbours and how appearances mattered to her and I'd thought – no, I'd assumed – that that was her primary motive for wanting to send me away when the reality was that she just didn't know how to be the kind of mother that I needed her to be.

But she did love me. She had said so.

I had been so stupid.

'Will we come back again?' A little voice beside me asked. I noticed that Mary didn't look up from the doll that she was playing with as she asked the question.

'Yes,' I said, 'I think we will.'

She nodded her head. 'I'm glad you and your mummy are friends again.'

So was I.

*** 

I phoned Mum the day after our first visit and she told me that Julie had had her baby just after midnight. It was a little boy and they were going to call him Michael. I told Mum that we'd see them on the weekend.

'We're looking forward to it,' Mum said and I believed her.

I couldn't wait to tell Mary that she had a new cousin. When she came out of school that day, instead of going straight home we went to the shops to buy the baby a present. I didn't have a lot of money but I managed to find a couple of T-shirts on a market stall. I let Mary choose them and she chose one that had an elephant on it and another with a teddy bear. She helped me wrap them up in blue tissue paper.

She'd been very confused about what had happened to Julie the day before and she'd asked me why Aunty Julie had wet herself all over Gran's sofa. I explained that she hadn't wet herself really, that it was just a sign that her baby was coming. She left it at that but I could tell that there was other stuff going on in her head. What got me the most about that conversation was how easily Mary had accepted my mum as 'Gran'. She'd never met the woman before and now it was like she had known her forever.

Mandy had been eager to hear all about our visit and she laughed her head off when I told her that the shock had sent Julie into labour. When I'd told her that we were going she'd tried to talk me out of it but now that the visit was over she said that she was glad it had gone well. I asked her if she thought she might contact her mum, but she said, 'No, probably not,' and I was sad for her.

She did contact her mum again but not until years later. And we've made lots more bus trips since then to see my parents and life has gone on, the way it does.

On one of those visits, we met Tim; well 'met' might be stretching it a bit. We walked past him and his mates as they were fixing a car.

Mary would have been about fifteen by then and it was funny in a way because she had asked about him not long before; she'd wanted to know what he was like. I wasn't very complimentary in my answers but Mary understood better after the day that we saw him.

It was one of his mates, Ben I think he was called, who saw us first and he said something to Tim and this other bloke and the next thing I knew they were all nudging each other and giggling like twelve-year-old schoolgirls. It was pathetic really and if I'd ever needed a reminder of the lucky escape I'd had, that was it.

I didn't have to tell Mary who he was because it must have been like looking in a mirror for her. She may have had my mother's eyes but the rest of her was pure Tim. She said something uncomplimentary about him herself and we carried on our way to my mum's house. I don't think I've ever heard her mention her dad since.

I didn't tell Mum or Dad about it because, even after all those years, it was still something that we didn't talk about. They loved Mary but how she'd come into their lives was sort of swept under the carpet.

Once, in the early days, Ida had stopped me in the street, got herself introduced to Mary and asked me if her dad was with us. It was a pretty poor attempt at getting the gossip because she only had to look at Mary to see who her dad was. I just said that he wasn't with us today and, 'Sorry, but we have to rush,' before making a quick escape.

'Lovely to see you again, Susan,' she called down the street. 'Nice to meet you, Mary.'

'What did she want?' Mum asked. She was at the door waiting for us.

'Nothing,' I said. 'She just wondered who Mary was.'

'What did you tell her?'

'That she was Mary.'

'Nosy cow.'

The words pot and kettle came to mind but I didn't say anything.

Ida was the only one of Mum's neighbours that ever asked about Mary's dad. She was the only one to pretend that she didn't really know what had happened. Some of the old neighbours had moved away in the years that I'd been gone and the rest didn't seem to care. They all had problems of their own. Ida's been dead a few years now though so no one asks about Mary's dad any more.

For a few months after the time we'd seen Tim, I'd half expected him to make some attempt to contact me but he never did. I thought maybe he might want to get to know his daughter. He must have known that Mary was his, one of many of his, from what I understand, living on the estate. Well, a few, at least. I don't know if he has any sort of relationship with any of them, but as time went on I was relieved that he apparently didn't want one with Mary either. I expect if he had come sniffing round she would have told him to get lost anyway. Mary knows that Tim has other children that she has half-siblings, but she has never shown any interest in finding out about them. She once called him her 'sperm donor' and I thought that was an adequate description. I was pleased she had no interest in him because, well, if I'm honest, Mary is *my* daughter.

***

Mary told me recently that I'm going to be a grandma and I couldn't be happier. She's been living with Jack for a few years and I think they've been trying for a baby for a while. I like Jack a lot. He has a good job and he works hard so I know he'll be able to provide for Mary and the baby but, more than that, he loves her – idolises her even. They are so happy together.

When Mum found out, she asked if they would be getting married but they won't be, not yet anyway. She says she doesn't understand the world and I suppose things must have been very different when she was young. I think she's looking forward to having a great-grandchild even though she says it makes her feel very old.

Mary had her scan today and found out that she is having a little girl. When I rang Mum to tell her she was going to have a great-granddaughter she asked if they had chosen any names yet.

'It won't be one of those daft names, will it? There's a lass down the road called her baby Aurora. Aurora, for God's sake. At least she'll be the only one in her class.'

I said I didn't know if they'd discussed names but I was fairly certain that Aurora wouldn't be high on the list.

Mary showed me the photograph of the baby girl that is still in her stomach and I was amazed. In my day we had scans but they were just images on a screen, something that only the mother saw. Now they are something that the whole family can enjoy.

Mary asked me if I had any advice for her and I told her that the best advice I could give her was to make sure that her child knew that she was loved, to enjoy every moment of her and to make sure that she puts ribbons her daughter's hair.

What can I say? Ribbons mean a lot to me.

## JEAN

Julie had said that she would get the door and I'd let her. I was peeling potatoes and my hands were filthy – I always buy the unwashed potatoes you see; they're a bit dirtier but what do you expect from something that's grown in the ground? They were always covered in dirt when I was young and I don't see the need to get someone else to wash my potatoes now.

Like I said, my hands were wet and dirty, so I let Julie get the door. We weren't expecting anyone so I strained my ears to hear who it was. Jehovah's Witnesses probably and they'd get short shrift from Julie. But there was no noise, not even the sound of the door closing so I dried my hands on a tea towel and popped my head out of the kitchen to look down the hallway. Julie was standing at the door looking out. She was holding on to the jamb like she was about to collapse or something. I was scared because she only had a couple of weeks to go before the baby came, so I went to see what was going on and who was at the door.

I got the shock of my life when I saw Susan standing there. She had the little one with her and the sight of her took

269

my breath away. She was like the spit out of Tim Preston's mouth. She had that same red tinge in her blonde hair and the same heart-shaped face. There was something about her eyes that didn't fit with the rest of her face but, apart from that, she was his. There was no denying that he was a good-looking lad but his daughter was stunning.

I brought them into the house and had a quick look in the street but luckily there was no one around. Not that I was so bothered by what the neighbours thought by then, but old habits die hard.

Those first few minutes were a bit awkward. I mean, what were we supposed to say to each other after all that time? The little one broke the ice by introducing herself and as I looked at her I thought to myself, *What the hell were you thinking, Jean? How could you have wanted to give this away?*

She was this tiny dot of a thing holding tight on to her mum with one hand and holding her other out for me to shake. I took hold of her hand and told her that I was her gran and for the first time in my life I knew what it felt like to instantly love something, or someone. I couldn't help myself. But I still had her mother to contend with and there was an awkward silence because I don't think either of us knew what to say.

I'd imagined seeing Susan again so many times and spent hours thinking about what I would say and do, but now that the moment had arrived all that went out the window. Julie took the little one away and left us to it.

I didn't say I was sorry – not then anyway – but I did say that I'd only been trying to do what I'd thought was best for her. And she said that so had she. There was a defiance about her that I hadn't seen before. She'd changed but I suppose that was only to be expected: she'd had to be strong for the little 'un. I said that Mary looked like a lovely little girl and Susan said that she had been worth everything. I didn't need to ask her what she meant by that; we both knew.

I know I'm an old woman now and it was such a long time ago but I'll never forget that day or how I felt. It was like the prodigal son returning home, except this time it was a daughter. I was so happy to see her. With all my heart I wished that I could hug her and tell her how happy I was to see her but that's not the type of person I am and I couldn't bring myself to do it, not right away. I needed more time.

Julie went into labour that day. Her waters broke while she was sitting on the sofa. Do you know, once upon a time I'd have been horrified about the mess but that day I couldn't have cared less. She had a little boy just after midnight and somehow I'd gained two grandchildren in one day.

271

Susan and I had a chance to talk after dinner when we were washing up. It was just the two of us so we were able to speak properly. I did manage to get the words out then and apologise and Susan seemed to accept it. Now she was a mother herself she was able to understand that I'd only been trying to do what I thought best for my child.

I was sorry when it was time for them to go. Just before they left, I finally got over the ridiculous hurdle that had been holding me back for so many years and I hugged my daughter. I just felt something pull me towards her. My God, it felt good! I wished that I had done it earlier, when she was little, but better late than never – isn't that what they say? I think I shocked her because it took a second or two for her to hug me back. And when she did, it was the best feeling in the world. I told her I loved her and she said that she loved me too … but I knew that already.

Susan didn't get to see Helen that day because they had to get the bus back. They couldn't stay over because they didn't have anything with them – I suppose she hadn't known how things would be when she arrived – and, anyway, Mary had school the next day. Helen got the shock of her life when I told her. She asked a few questions but she didn't say much, though she did say that she was worried about Julie.

We'd been drinking brandy when Helen and Richard came round later that evening and I don't think Helen was very impressed. She didn't say anything, but you could just tell. I didn't care though; we were celebrating.

Mick was a different person after Susan came back. He had his princess again and so he was happy. He adored Mary from the moment he saw her ... no, what am I saying? He'd adored her since he'd known she was born, long before he ever met her. She was Susan's child and that made her special. It didn't matter how many grandchildren he had in the future, Mary would always be special, just like her mum.

I was happy too. Mick had always said she would come back and I was glad that he was right I just couldn't show it like he did. I knew I was going to have to learn how to show my emotions but, if I'm honest, I've never really got the hang of it.

Julie was over the moon to have her sister back. They hadn't been close when they were young but they'd turned a corner just before it all kicked off and, to give Julie her due, she'd always been on Susan's side. Helen seemed happy enough but she's more like me and didn't show what she was feeling. She'd always been the most independent of the three and she still kept herself to herself a lot of the time. I'd blamed Robert's mother for the way she'd been with us over

273

the years but maybe it had just been the way she was. Richard was good for her though, so I wasn't worried about her.

Susan and Mary have never come back to live here but they have been regular visitors and when Susan got a phone of her own we rang each other regularly; we'd speak a couple of times a week. At last I was having a relationship with my daughter and I kicked myself over all the time that we had lost. I blamed myself for it; I knew I hadn't been the kind of mother that Susan wanted, that she needed. I saw the way that she was with her own daughter – the cuddles, the kisses, the secret looks that only they understood – and I was jealous. Susan was the type of mother that I wished I could have been if only things had been different.

But what was done was done and there was nothing I could do about it. All I could do was try to be different from then on and though it's not been easy for me to be that type of person I think I'm getting better at it.

Mary was a lovely girl, a credit to her mother, but I still couldn't get away from the feeling that because of her Susan didn't have the kind of life that she could have had. Of all my girls, Susan was the one that could have done something with her life, made something of herself, but instead she was still alone and living in a council house with a daughter who was the image of a man that didn't want her. I'd told her that no man would want her when she had another man's child. It gave me no pleasure to be right, but it didn't seem to bother Susan. What was it that she had said though, the day she came back and we were standing in the hallway? She'd said that it had all been worth it. Susan had been many things but a liar wasn't one of them.

I often wondered what she thought when she looked at Mary, who must have been a constant reminder to her of, well, you-know-who, but I never asked her and she never said.

They passed in the street once. Mary would have been a teenager by then but she had lost none of her father's looks. I was in the front bedroom when I heard a lot of noise outside. Tim was just down the street with Ben Morris and that lad that had just moved in with his wife and two kids. They were all standing by a car, carrying on, laughing and joking, while someone was underneath the car fixing it. I couldn't see who it was but if I'd had to guess I'd say it was Ben's brother Daniel because he was always fiddling with cars. Anyway, I knew that Susan and Mary were due so I'd gone upstairs into the front bedroom so I could watch for them coming. I wondered if I should tell Mick so that he could go and meet them but it was too late for that; they were already coming round the corner. My heart was in my mouth.

I couldn't hear what was being said but it was obvious that they had been seen. Ben and the other lad started nudging and pushing Tim and even through the closed window I could hear them laughing. I was so proud of Susan when she just kept her head up, looked forward and walked on past. She didn't even acknowledge him.

I think that is the only time that Mary has ever seen her dad.

I think that was also the year that James went off to university; that was a first for this family. Helen had never had any more children so she doted on James and it broke her heart to see him go. I tried telling her that it was a good thing but she just cried and then she cried a bit more.

I'm too old for these dramas and I told her so. 'It's not like you didn't know he was going,' I said. 'You've had time to prepare. Anyway, I thought you wanted him to go. You'll see him again in a few weeks.'

I know that she thought I was being heartless but I was just telling her the truth. It wasn't like he was disappearing into the night never to be seen again for years.

He's finished university since then and got a job the other side of London so she doesn't see much of him now either;

none of us do. She'll see even less next year. He's marrying a Spanish girl and going to live in Madrid. At least she'll get cheap holidays.

Julie and Chris are just the same as always. They are like two peas in a pod, made for each other. They only had Michael but that doesn't seem to matter to them. He's twenty now and training to be some sort of engineer.

And then there's Mary. She works in an office somewhere and lives with Jack and he seems like a nice enough bloke. They're having a baby. Susan rang last night and told me.

'You're going to be a great grandma,' she told me and I cried. They're not planning on getting married – nobody seems to get married these days; they're all living over the brush – but there's nothing I can do about it, so I don't worry. The world has changed a lot since I was a girl.

So, Susan is going to be a grandma before she's forty. She's still alone though, just like I said she would be. That worries me sometimes but it's the bed she chose to lie in and she seems happy enough with her lot.

## HELEN

I didn't know what was going on when we got to Mum's house that night. She and Dad were sitting in the living room chatting away to each other like I hadn't seen them do in years. Richard and I had heard the laughter as soon as we'd come through the door and we'd looked at each other as if to say *what the hell* ...? The noise woke James up. He'd been half asleep on my shoulder and at seven he was a bit heavy to be carrying but he'd fallen asleep in the car so I'd had no choice. He didn't really want to wake up but the sound of what I can only describe as raucous laughter woke him right up.

Richard took James from me and I carefully opened the frosted glass door to the living room. I wondered what I'd see when I got inside but it turned out to be just Mum and Dad sitting next to each other on the sofa with a bottle of brandy and two half-filled glasses on the coffee table in front of them.

Mum saw me out of the corner of her eye. 'Come on in,' she said waving us over. 'You too, Richard, come on in – we have got so much to tell you.'

'What is it? Oh, happy Mother's Day,' I said, 'holding out the gift bag that was hooked on my little finger. 'Sorry we couldn't make lunch and I know we're late but the traffic was ridiculous.' I sat down in one chair and Richard sat in the other with James on his knee. 'Has Julie gone?' I asked. It was a daft question because she obviously wasn't there.

'Aye,' Mum giggled, 'gone into labour.'

'Labour? Is she all right?'

'Yes,' Mum said, without the giggle this time which I was thankful for because frankly it didn't suit her. She was a like a stranger.

With her emotions under control she told me that Julie's waters had broken that afternoon, right there on the sofa. That explained the towel that was across one of the seats. Chris had rung from the hospital about an hour earlier to say things were progressing as they should be. I was just wondering if they had been this excited when I went into labour with James when Dad told me the real reason for the celebration.

'Susan came back,' he said.

I thought I'd misheard him at first. I mean, why would Susan come back? But I only had to look at Dad's face to know that he was telling the truth. I'd never seen him look so

279

happy. I didn't know what to say and, in the end, all I could do was ask, 'When?'

'Today,' he said. 'She just turned up out of the blue on the doorstep.'

'With the little girl?' I asked.

'Yes, with Mary,' Mum said, without even a hint of embarrassment.

Mum had become more tolerant of people in recent years and anyway, a pregnant teenager wasn't her shame du jour any more was it? Susan and her secret were out of sight now, unlike my divorce. Except they were back suddenly and Mum seemed quite happy about it. Maybe she had changed more than I had given her credit for.

I asked where Susan was now and they said that she'd gone home. I asked where home was and was surprised when they told me. It had a good shopping centre on the outskirts where Robert and I used to do our Christmas shopping. Had I ever come close to seeing her?

I was happy that Susan was back, really I was, but I just couldn't understand it. Why then? What had changed? I got the chance to ask her the following week when she came again but I didn't bother; it didn't make any difference did it? What mattered was that she was back with the daughter that was the image of all of Tim Preston's kids. Apart form the eyes that is – the eyes weren't his.

I'd spent all week wondering how I would react when I saw her. We'd never been close, in fact I used to try and ignore her to tell you the truth. When I was young I was a bit embarrassed by her I think though I don't really know why. It might have been the greasy hair and the chubby cheeks but I'd like to think that I'm not that shallow. I was going to have to face her again and I didn't know what to expect.

When I saw her she just opened her arms up and I couldn't help but go into them. I'd never hugged her before in my life – I'm not big into physical contact – but she was hugging me so what could I do? We didn't say much to each other, so there was nothing new there, but we did exchange pleasantries. I introduced her to Richard and she introduced us to Mary. The child was perfectly pleasant and so well mannered. I had to admit that she could have taught James a thing or two, especially the words please and thank you.

The next time I met up with Susan was the afternoon that we all went round to Julie's. She'd just come out of hospital after having her baby and I remember thinking there we were, three sisters with our children. How different things were since the last time we'd all been together.

We're still not close, not as close as she and Julie are but I am glad that Susan came back into our lives. She's going to be a grandma soon and I can't help wishing it was me.

**JULIE**

Mum was busy in the kitchen with the dinner so I'd said that I would get the door. There was football on and Dad and Chris were watching it, so if we'd waited for them to answer the knock whoever it was would have been standing there a long time. I don't know who I'd expected to find on a Sunday lunchtime but if I'd had to guess I would never have said Susan. Yet there she was.

I'd always thought it was a cliché when people said that their hearts were in their mouths but no, it's real; I know it can happen because that's exactly what happened to me. Suddenly something was thumping in my throat and I felt faint. I had to lean against the door jamb to stop myself falling over. Time sort of stood still for a minute and the next thing I knew, Mum was standing beside me face to face with the daughter she hadn't seen for ... how long was it? Six years?

Once I'd got over the initial shock I was so happy to see her. And the little one of course; my God, she was the spit of Tim, apart from the eyes that is, there was something about the eyes. Mum told them to come in and shut the door. There was a bit of a stand off between Mum and Susan; they are as stubborn as each other and I didn't know who was going to blink first. Then Mary introduced herself to her grandma which took Mam by surprise and then Mam surprised me even more by telling her that she was her gran. Mam had a bit of a wobble on when she took Mary's hand but she soon pulled herself together and she and Susan started looking at each other again. I suggested that I take Mary to meet her granddad so that the pair of them could get on with whatever they were going to do. I don't think Mary was that keen on leaving her mum, which was hardly surprising given that she didn't know me from Adam and she could probably sense the tension, but Susan gave her the nod and she went with me into the living room.

Chris had a look of *who is that?* On his face but Dad knew exactly who it was immediately. His face lit up as soon as he saw her.

'Is…?' He didn't get any further than that.

I nodded my head and took Mary to him. God love her, she offered her hand for him to shake and said, 'Hello, I'm Mary and I am very pleased to meet you.' It was adorable.

Dad took her hand and said he was pleased to meet her too. He looked at me and I could see the question that was on

284

his face. I nodded my head to the door that I had just come through just to reassure him that Susan was here too.

He sobbed when Susan came into the room. She sobbed too and they hugged each other for a long time. They've always had a special bond and it was as though, now they were back together, they didn't want to let each other go. Mum watched them and whereas before there would have been something critical on her face now she smiled. Mum really had changed and it was only then that I realised how much.

I didn't get the chance to enjoy the reunion though because they'd been there less than half an hour when I felt something warm and wet and realised that my waters had broken. I thought *bloody hell, I'm sitting on Mum's sofa* but it wasn't like it was something I could hide so I had to come clean and tell her I was sorry. She told me not to be so soft and that it couldn't be helped! It was like an alien had taken over her body. Mum rang the hospital and then Chris and I had to leave.

I didn't know how to feel about the baby coming. I was excited obviously. I – we – had wanted this baby so much and now it was on its way, but I also wanted to talk to Susan. I had a million questions that I wanted to ask her but my priority was my baby, just as Susan's had been, so I went off

285

to hospital and Susan promised that she would come and see me the following week.

Chris will tell you that I talked about Susan all the way through my labour. Obviously he knew what had happened that had made her go away but he didn't know much about what her childhood had been like. I told him how hard I think it was for her being so much younger than Helen and me. We'd had each other but she was on her own. She didn't even have Mum; none of us had really but it seemed worse for Susan. I told Chris something that I had never admitted to anyone not even him before; I told him that I wished things had been different, that I had been a better sister to her when she was young. The trouble was that even though I tried to appear like a bolshy teenager I was easily led by Helen. She was the older sister and I had always looked up to her so I followed her lead when it came to Susan. Plus, like I said, she was so much younger than us that we didn't have a lot in common. We became closer after Helen married Robert and then I wished that we'd done it earlier. She was a good kid and things might have been different.

Anyway, things were what they were, and at least we had found the relationship that we should have always had. And thank God we did; she'd felt able to contact me after she'd left and I think if she hadn't been able to do that we might not have heard from her ever again.

I always hoped that she'd come back but I hadn't expected it to happen that day. And what a day that was! I had my son Michael just after midnight. It was the happiest day of my life.

Susan was true to her word and came back to see me the following week. I'd just got home from hospital the day before when Helen and Susan came to visit me in the afternoon. They both had their children with them and it felt really good that the three of us were together with our little ones. It was something I hadn't dared to hope would happen. Chris took a picture of the six of us. I haven't looked at it in a while but I have it somewhere.

Mary was a credit to Susan. I'd liked her as soon as I saw her but as I got to know her I liked her even more. That day, the one just after Michael was born, she gave me a little parcel that was wrapped up in blue tissue paper and said that it was a present for the baby. There were two T-shirts inside, one had an elephant on I remember, and I was so grateful. I knew money must be tight for Susan and her gesture, their gesture, really touched me. She'd already forked out for the bus fares twice and she'd still somehow managed to find the money for a gift for Michael. Mind, she always could save, not like me; I spend it as soon as I get it. I suppose she'd had to get used to managing her money.

Mum had started to change before Susan came back but I noticed the difference in her even more afterwards. I think she still cared what the neighbours thought but she blocked them out now, she was just glad to have her daughter back. She never talked about what had happened though, not to me anyway and I doubt she has to Susan. We as a family never spoke about who Mary's father was, why Susan did what she did, or any of it really. It was something we all knew had happened but we just didn't acknowledge it, if that makes sense.

I often wish that Susan had moved back but she never has. She says that she likes where she lives, that she has friends there and that she is happy, and that's what matters the most. We see a lot of her though and I talk to her on the phone two or three times a week.

I don't think she has ever bothered with another man or at least, if she has, she's never mentioned it to me. Mum always said that a man wouldn't be interested in her once she had a baby. I'm not sure Mary is the reason Susan is still alone though, not in the way Mum meant. Mary is all that Susan needs.

And now that she's going to be a grandma she is so happy and I'm happy for her.

## MARY

I love my mum so much. She's more than a parent to me, she's a friend too. She's my best friend.

Mum risked everything so that I could be born. She'd become pregnant as a teenager and ran away from home for reasons I'm not quite sure of, though I suspect it has something to do with my grandmother. She lived in a hostel for unmarried mothers in the months leading up to my birth and we lived a series of council houses after that.

When Mum tells me of those very early days when we lived in a one bedroom flat she always smiles. I think that we were happy there. She's told me all about the people that lived near us and I wish that I could remember them, especially the lady called Miriam because Mum seems very fond of her. Apparently she used to sing a lot. Mum's friend Mandy also lived a few doors away from us with her daughter Jade but I don't remember that either. I mean I've known them all of my life and they were always dropping into our house, or we were in theirs; I just can't remember that flat, but then I was only about two when we moved so I suppose it's not surprising.

When I was five, Mum decided that we were going to visit her parents and we went on Mother's Day. I don't know if I actually remember what happened that day or if it's something that I think I remember because I've been told the story so often. I vaguely remember the bus journey. It seemed really long but I didn't mind because riding on the bus was an adventure to me.

I do remember the way they looked at me though, these people that were my family. It was like they weren't sure if I was real or not. I don't remember much else about that day apart from the fact that one of the people, the one that turned out to be my Aunty Julie, wet herself and had to go to hospital because she said that her baby was coming. Of course she hadn't wet herself, it was her waters breaking, but as a five-year-old I just thought she'd had a really big wee on the sofa and I remember being very confused by how that meant she was going to have a baby. I hadn't wet myself in ages but that day I resolved always to go to the toilet as soon as I felt the need – I am so embarrassed to admit that and I can't believe I've told you but I've said it to you now so I can't take it back.

Aunty Julie had a baby boy and called him Michael after his granddad. Mum explained to me that my auntie's baby was my cousin and that I had another cousin too. In addition to the cousins I had grandparents, two aunts and even an uncle. However in all of this family there was no mention of a father. I think I was about eight when I asked Mum about him. She said that they just hadn't got along and that she'd decided to bring me up on her own. That was enough for me when I was a very a small girl but as I got older I started to ask more questions. Not so much about why he wasn't around but rather who he was. Did he know about me? What was he like? Was I like him? Her answers were, 'No.' 'A prat' and 'Yes, I did look like him.'

I met him when I was about fifteen. Well, I didn't meet him exactly but I saw him in the street. He was with a couple of other men standing around a car watching a fourth man fiddle about underneath it. He gave Mum a double take as we walked past and muttered something to his mates that I couldn't hear. They all burst out laughing and started nudging each other. Mum kept her eyes straight ahead and marched past them towards my grandparents' house. I looked at her as I walked beside her and I saw the muscles in the side of her face twitching as though it was taking everything she had to behave the way she was.

'That was him, wasn't it?' I said and she barely nodded her head. I linked arms with her and said, 'I think you were being generous when you called him a prat.' We both laughed.

She didn't have to ask how I knew who he was because she had been right when she said I looked like him; it was like looking in a mirror. His face was my face. I thought that made my mum even more remarkable than I'd already thought she was because she loved me despite the fact that when she saw me she must have seen him.

After that day I understood my grandmother's behaviour towards me a bit more. Clearly I reminded her of the man who did my mother wrong – her words not mine. My gran was never hostile towards me, in fact she was lovely but, I don't know, I always got the feeling that there was something different about me compared to her other grandchildren. The way I looked didn't put my granddad off though; he always made me feel special but I think that was because Mum is so special to him.

I've never missed having a dad. When I was very young I didn't know what one was so I didn't know what I was missing and, as I got older – I don't know how to explain it – I just didn't feel like I was missing out on anything. I do feel sorry for Mum though. She's on her own at home now and she must get lonely. She says she isn't but there are only so many books you can read. I've never known her go out with a man. It's like my dad – or 'the sperm donor' as I prefer to think of him – poisoned her against all men and I'm sorry about that. I don't like the idea of her being lonely because of me. She's still young so maybe there's still time for her to meet Mr Right. I hope so.

Like mother like daughter, as they say, I recently found myself unmarried and pregnant. At twenty-two I'm older than Mum was and my baby is planned. I've lived with Jack for almost three years and we've been trying for a baby for the last eighteen months or so. We think we'll get married one day but not right now.

When I told Mum I was pregnant she couldn't have been more pleased. She threw her arms around me and told me how happy she was for me and Jack. I am pretty sure that was the exact opposite to the reaction Mum had when she'd delivered the same news to her own mother all those years ago. The sad thing was that when I told my gran that I was having a baby she was happy for me. Not doing cartwheels happy, but happy enough in her own way. She even knitted cardigans for the baby … lots of cardigans.

After my twenty-week scan I couldn't wait to show Mum the picture of my baby, this little thing, clearly human but not quite fully formed, curled up tightly in a ball. Mum cried as she looked at the photograph and so did I.

'Did you ask them if it was a boy or a girl?' Mum asked me.

I'd thought that I wouldn't want to find out the sex of our baby but Jack had wanted to know and when push came to shove I'd decided I did too. 'It's a girl,' I told her.

Mum sat leaning forward, resting her elbows on her knees. She held the photo in one of her shaking hands and had her other hand clasped firmly over her mouth. I knew that she was smiling because I could see it in her eyes.

'What advice would you give me, Mum, on bringing up a little girl?' I was being flippant and hadn't expected a serious answer.

But I got one anyway.

She took her hand away from her mouth and reached out to me. I shuffled forward in my own seat so that we could reach each other and hold hands.

'Enjoy every minute,' she said, 'make her feel loved and … ribbons.' Mum locked her eyes on to mine. 'Ribbons,' she said again. 'Make sure you put ribbons in her hair.'

## ACKNOWLEDGEMENTS

A little girl with long blonde hair tied up in a red ribbon started a conversation that sparked the idea for this book. My thanks go to the little girl, who I do not know, and to the person I spoke to, who I will not name – they know who they are.

I am always thankful to my parents and siblings for making my childhood special. I had no idea that all children didn't grow up with the love that I did.

John, John and Andrew aka 'my men,' are the reason that I get up in the morning. You are the reason behind everything that I do. I love you all very much and wouldn't be here without you.

Thank you to my fellow writers for your support over the years – it has been invaluable. Also, to my dear friend Jan Weiss for your encouragement over the (many) years that we have known each other. You are the one person who knows exactly what it has taken me to get here.

Special thanks have to go to the staff of Sunderland Royal Hospital, especially the renal unit, ICCU and ward

297

B28. You saved my life and made me healthy again so I will never be able to thank you enough.

I would like to thank the wonderful people at Accent Press for making this possible. I especially thank Hazel Cushion for publishing the book, as well as for giving advice and encouragement whenever I needed it. I would also like to thank Katrin Lloyd for all the tips around promotion and for answering the many, and often stupid, questions that I threw at her. Finally, thank you to my editor Penny Hunter for making this book the best it could be and for keeping the timeline in check.

If I have forgotten anyone please accept my apologies.

Proudly published by Accent Press

www.accentpress.co.uk